BROTHERHOOD
OF THE
GOAT

ISBN-13: 978-1-63696-168-2
ISBN-10: 1-63696-168-1

Cover design by: Damonza
Printed in the United States of America

DAVID ARCHER
BLAKE BANNER

BROTHERHOOD
OF THE
GOAT

AN ALEX
MASON
THRILLER

R
RIGHT HOUSE

ALEX MASON SERIES

PROLOGUE

Frazer Benson thought he was immortal. Especially when he took his red capsule. When he was drunk, he was sure he was immortal. Right now, he was drunk. He had been at Jack Magnuson's eighty-sixth birthday party, he had taken two of the reds, and he had drunk enough to float the fleet.

He was in his Bentley Continental convertible cruising up Sunset Boulevard through Holmby Hills, remembering the press of glittering people. The people sparkled more than the diamonds they were wearing. There was every goddamned star in Hollywood there. You *had* to be there. If you weren't there, pal, you were nobody. And *he* had been there. He laughed out loud to the sky. He, Frazer Benson, had been there. Not only had he been there, he had been invited personally by Jack Magnuson himself. The man who was going to be honored at the next Oscars as the greatest cinema actor of the twentieth and the twenty-first centuries. That was the man who had invited him to his eighty-sixth birthday party.

He came to the big intersection with Benedict Canyon Drive. The lights were red for him, but he cut across anyway into Hartford Way. He heard a couple of horns behind him, gave them the finger, and laughed.

"Screw you!" he screamed. *"I got invited to Jack*

Magnuson's birthday party! Losers!"

He chuckled. He knew it was childish, but he didn't give a damn. He was a god.

He pulled up at his gate. He knew there was nobody at home. His wife was at her mother's. He thought about getting a couple of hookers, but he was tired. It was four a.m., and there was the risk his wife would come back before they'd left. The gate rolled open, and he rolled in. Then it rolled closed behind him with a big clang.

He didn't bother putting the car in the garage. Suddenly he was tired and just wanted a nightcap and bed. He climbed from his car and walked, a little unsteadily, across the lawn to the big oak front door flanked by the marble columns he had imported personally from Persia. He liked to think of it as Persia when he thought about his columns. They had once belonged to a Persian king, after all. He chuckled as he fit his key into the lock. Persia made carpets and marble columns. Iran was a place you bombed.

He noticed absently that there was a dim light in his drawing-room window. That was odd because his wife was not home. His wife called it the living room, but his mother had taught him that common people live in their living rooms, whereas people with class withdraw to the drawing room. He let himself in. The door closed behind him with a heavy clunk. He hung up his coat and his scarf and entered the drawing room, undoing his bowtie and telling himself he was definitely not common.

He had reached the credenza and was pouring himself a twenty-one-year-old Bushmills single malt when he became aware, by some sixth sense, that somebody was sitting watching him from the couch by the window, under the standard lamp. He turned.

He could see the legs, the very shiny black shoes, and the slender white hands, but the face and the body were in shadow.

"Who the hell—"

"You weren't expecting me."

The voice was disembodied, emerging from the dark. It wasn't a question. It was more like an observation. The voice was quiet, almost melodious. Frazer frowned.

"You..."

"Tom called me."

"Tom?"

"He said you were talking to Melanie Westwood."

"Yeah." Frazer pointed to the silver tray of decanters. "You want a drink?"

"No. She is a wonderful actress. The best, in my book. She and Magnuson dominated the twentieth century. Real artists. Shame they only made two movies together." Frazer nodded, gaping slightly, half listening but mainly wondering what the hell was going on. The voice said, "She refused to work with him, you know. He's a genius, but he's an animal, a Hell's Angel turned movie star. That's why Humberto loves him." A quiet laugh. "He was all over her, making sexual advances, groping her. She's a lady. An elegant woman." A pause. "But magnetic, electrifying, sensual—" He paused again, giving meaning to his next words. "The kind of woman any man would want to impress."

Frazer lowered himself into a chair. "Uh, Lou, you know it's always a pleasure to see you guys—"

"No."

"Huh...?" Frazer's eyes went wide and he smiled.

"It is not always a pleasure to see us, Frazer. Sometimes we torture people."

He laughed. "You *what?*"

There was a subtle shift in the voice. It was still soft, still quiet, but now there was a relentless, unforgiving hardness to it. "We explain very clearly at the beginning that there are absolute red lines. Stay within the lines and the benefits can be unlimited, but you do not cross the lines."

"Sure, but—"

"You don't cross the lines, Frazer. If you cross the lines, just as the benefits of obedience are potentially unlimited, so the punishment for crossing the lines can be unlimited. Sometimes we torture people."

The smile had melted from Frazer's face like warm wax. He had gone pale, and there was a hot pellet of fear in his belly that made him want to vomit.

"Listen, but I didn't—"

"Tom told us what you did and what you didn't do. He heard your conversation and he felt the need to intervene. I am going to ask you. Frazer. What would have happened, what would you have told Melanie, if he had not butted into your conversation?"

"No, nothing. I just said—"

"I know what you said, Frazer. Tom told me."

"But it was nothing. I—"

"It wasn't nothing, Frazer. It was a red line, and you crossed it."

A soft noise behind him made him turn. There were two men. They both wore expensive dark gray suits. They both had black bags over their heads. Absurdly he wondered how they could see. Lou laughed out loud.

"Relax, Frazer! Come on! We're family! We are not going to hurt you. I just wanted to scare you a bit. Consider this a first warning. If it happens again, things will be a lot more serious."

Frazer laughed once, too loud, then relaxed into his chair with his heart pounding.

"You guys. If what you wanted was to scare me, you sure succeeded!"

It was as he said "succeeded" that he felt the sharp bee sting in his arm. He turned, frowning, and saw that it was not a bee, but a syringe. The needle had penetrated his jacket sleeve and his shirt and plunged deep into his arm. His arm throbbed. He tried to move it, but the guy with the black cloth bag on his head was holding down his wrist. On the other side, the other guy was doing the same. He turned to Lou. Lou stood and came out of the shadows. His long, thin, pale face was smiling. He came and hunkered down in front of Frazer, one long, thin hand on each knee.

"You remember I said we were not going to hurt you?"

Frazer tried to nod, but the impulse never reached his muscles.

"It's a distillation of curare. It paralyzes your muscles but does not rob you of feeling. You can still feel the whole, rich range of sensations." His smile broadened. It seemed to Frazer to be full of sharp, terrifying angles, his mouth like an arrow tip pointing down, his nose like a dagger, his eyes like two blades. "But I told you, didn't I, that we would not hurt you." He drew his face so close to Fraser's that their noses were touching, and his slit eyes penetrated into Frazer's, his breath stinking in Frazer's

5

nose. His voice, when it came, was a vicious rasp. *"Well, I lied, Frazer, because we are going to hurt you a lot!"*

ONE

Nero put a grape in his mouth and chewed, then sipped his Armagnac, a Bas Armagnac de Gaube, from the appellation contrôlée Corderoy du Tiers.

"Really," he said, doing a lot of vaguely unpleasant stuff with his mouth, "really very good. Rare. Hard to get hold of. Extremely good."

I watched him and waited with a smile that never made it past my nose. When he had finally smacked his lips and reached for another grape, I spoke.

"Sir, when somebody, even an actress, even a great actress and a Hollywood star, reports a murder, that is an FBI matter. That's not our jurisdiction."

He froze halfway through a chew and arched an eyebrow at me. I cleared my throat. "Obviously you know that. So I am guessing there must be some good reason why you want me to travel to Los Angeles and talk to Melanie Westwood."

He finished his chew. "That would not be an unreasonable assumption, Alex." He sipped his Armagnac and leaned back in his chair while he savored it. "First, we have no jurisdictional limits. Second, Miss Westwood approached the Federal Bureau of

Investigation a week ago, a few days after hearing of the death of Frazer Benson. Mr. Benson was an acquaintance of hers. They had many friends and acquaintances in common. I believe," he said, twitching his considerable nose over the rim of his glass, "that the Hollywood star world is an incestuous and narcissistic one. They wish to be seen and adored, and their friends are all simply status symbols, as are their cars, houses, and clothes with particular labels. Their world is made up, then, of those people and things with which they wish to be associated."

"Well, that pretty much disposes of them."

He ignored me. "Frazer Benson was one of those people with whom one wished to be associated. He had recently become a billionaire. He was both a financier and an extremely expensive consultant on investments."

"So what happened, he gave some bad advice and somebody got mad? Or some husband didn't appreciate Benson advising his wife in his bedroom?"

"Mr. Benson was at Jack Magnuson's birthday party just over a week ago. He was apparently a close friend of Mr. Magnuson's. While there, Mr. Benson apparently got into conversation with Melanie Westwood. She claimed he was drunk and, in her words, 'talked a lot of bullshit.' Shortly after that conversation, he left and went home, where he was murdered some time shortly after four a.m."

"You know the time because the security cameras on his gate recorded the time of his arrival."

"Correct."

"Sir, not that I don't enjoy your narrative style— in fact, I was just thinking you really ought to be on the radio with that voice—but I have two questions. First, what makes this a federal case? Why are the Feds involved at all? And, more to the point, what makes it even remotely interesting for us?"

"That is three questions, Alex."

"Yes, sir. I'll boil it down to one. This is a simple murder investigation with no federal angle and no national security angle, so why are we interested?"

"Reserve your judgment until you have all the facts. You will fly to Los Angeles and pay a visit to Miss Westwood on Moraga Drive, in Bel-Air. Listen to her story. You may change your mind." He reached into his drawer, pulled out a small manila envelope, and dropped it in front of me. "You will be Special Agent Alex Mason. Your badge and other identification is in there. Take the company plane. If I am right, which of course I am, we do not want to be wasting time."

* * *

Some two thousand three hundred miles away, deep in a valley in Bel-Air, not a mile from the Getty View Park, a tall, thin man in a dark gray suit parked his anonymous, metallic gray Toyota Camry outside the large gate on Moraga Drive and walked to the video-entryphone, where he pressed call and looked up at the camera so it could see his face. It was a long, thin face.

A woman's voice answered, asking who he was. He pulled a Federal Bureau of Investigation badge from his inside pocket, opened it, held it up to be seen clearly by the camera, and enunciated, "Jeremiah Brown, Federal Bureau of Investigation. I'd like to ask Ms. Westwood a few questions. May I come in?"

There was a pause for maybe fifteen seconds, then the gate buzzed and opened. He looked up at the camera again, smiled and raised a hand in thanks, then walked in on long, thin legs.

He was met at the door by Isabel, who showed him through a large, terracotta-tiled entrance hall to a spacious living room with a bare, redbrick fireplace and low bookcases against every wall.

The voice made him start and turn. Melanie Westwood stood in jeans and a sweatshirt addressing her maid. "Isa, bring some lemonade, please." She stopped and smiled at the man. "Unless you would like something else."

He stared at her for a moment, smiling. His mouth was like a large V, she thought, into which his sharp nose fit perfectly. But his eyes, like two crescents, were an unnerving pale blue.

"No!" he said suddenly. "Lemonade, what could be better on a sunny day like this?"

She gestured to a chair. "Please, won't you sit?"

"Thank you." He sat, still staring at her with his mouth slightly open. "Forgive me, it must be tedious for you. I bet you hear it all the time. But I am a great admirer of your work. So versatile. I always think you must have such empathy to be able to understand such a wide variety of characters."

"Oh." He watched with pleasure as her cheeks colored. She spread her hands. "It's a craft. But I'm sure you didn't come here to talk about my work. How can I help you, Special Agent Brown?"

"I know you have been over this already, and I am sorry to burden you with more questions. The thing is, you see, we are conducting a separate investigation involving international trade, liquid assets, and money laundering." He waved his hand, suggesting it was all boring, complicated stuff. "But we have reason to believe Mr. Benson's death may be connected."

"I see. Well, by all means ask, but I am not sure I can tell you anything I didn't tell your colleagues."

Isabel came in with a large glass jug of bright yellow lemonade that clinked with ice. She placed it on the table beside Melanie and withdrew while Melanie filled two glasses. He rose, on his long, thin legs to take the glass she offered him.

"What I am really most interested in, Miss Westwood, is what, precisely, in as much detail as you can, Mr. Benson told you at the party."

She took a deep breath and gazed out of the window. Her bright red rosebushes were there, and she would really much rather have been tending to them than talking to this man, with his long, thin legs.

"He was pretty incoherent," she said. "He was talking about some club he belonged to in France. He said the members were all politicians, high-ranking European Union officials, judges, and billionaires."

"Did he say where in France?"

She thought for a moment. "I'm not sure. He said something about the region of Occitanie, Coudrey? South of Foix. He said the club was at a castle. He said the castle had an Occitan name rather than French." She paused to think. "Castèl de Coudrey? It was something like that."

The man chortled as he made notes. "The fantasies of some people. Did he say what kind of things they got up to at this club?"

"My impression at first was that he was trying to impress me. He made it sound like the Bilderberg Group or the Illuminati. They all got together to smoke cigars and drink cognac and manipulate international affairs."

"Anything specific or particular?"

She studied the man's face for a moment. It was something about his eyes. She shook her head.

"No. As I say, the impression I had at the time was that it was all bullshit. Frazer was fabulously rich, but he never got tired of telling you. He was a very insecure man who needed to boast and conquer all the time. He'd been hitting on me for a long time. I assumed that was what he was doing then. Trying to impress me. As I told your colleague, I only approached you because it was that same night..."

She trailed off. Agent Brown said, "That he was killed."

"Yes."

"You certainly did the right thing. It is probably as you say, just showing off, but because of his connections and the amount of money he made in the last couple of years, we have to look into it."

"Sure."

She sipped, and he watched her in silence. She drew breath to ask him if there was anything else, but he cut her short. "Many people like Mr. Benson are so foolish. A man in his position, carrying the responsibility of so much wealth, his responsibility to his clients, and his contacts, a man like that should not drink and boast. He should be modest and mature. And discreet. Do you not think so, Ms. Westwood?"

She didn't answer. He went on, "Take a woman of your own substantial wealth and achievement. So many people depend on you. Not just your employees, but friends and family. But you, you see, have the wisdom of your considerable intelligence and experience in life. And that makes you discreet."

She frowned and set down her half-empty glass. "I am not sure—"

"Indiscretion," he said as though she had not spoken. "Indiscretion costs lives, and what is worse, it costs pain. Pain to the indiscreet, to those who love them, and those they love."

"Special Agent Brown—"

"I mean," he said, setting down his glass, untouched, "look at the way poor Mr. Benson died. It is hard for most of us to imagine what he went through, but to a woman with such empathy as you have, it must be an awful thing to imagine. If only he had been discreet, it might never have happened."

He stood. He seemed very tall as she looked up at his thin, gray face and his pale eyes. She tried to speak, but fear had constricted her throat.

"Please, don't get up, I don't want to take your time. Time is so precious. I am sure it was just as you said. He was just showing off to a beautiful, desirable lady. I should just forget the whole thing if I were you."

"Yes," she said. "I—" Her mouth was dry, and she licked her lips. "I am sure you're right." She laughed. It was a strained, humorless laugh. "It was just a silly, drunken episode. It's fading from my mind as we speak."

"That's right, Ms Westwood. That's the ticket. Goodbye."

He turned and walked away on his long, thin legs, with his strange, almost loping stride. She heard the door close, rose, and hurried to the kitchen, where she and Isa watched him on the camera as he crossed the sidewalk to his car. The lights flashed, and he reached for the handle of the driver's door. There he paused, turned, and smiled straight at them. He opened the door, climbed in, and reversed away.

"Who was that man, *señora*? I don' like him."

She didn't answer but turned and made her way back to the living room, where she stood staring at her blood-red roses through the window.

"*Señora*?"

She turned and saw Isa in the door, holding a cloth too tightly with both hands. She gave a small, quiet laugh.

"It was nothing, Isa. Just a rather strange agent from the FBI." She looked back at the window and spoke half to herself. "If you hadn't seen him too, I might have thought I had dreamed it."

* * *

Not a mile away, Lou was giggling in his car. He wished he had somebody he could phone and tell, but since his mother had died back at the turn of the millennium, he had had nobody to talk to or confide in. But that didn't mean he couldn't pretend. He hunched his shoulders and grinned.

"Beep beep beep, beep beep beep, beep beep, beep beep." He paused a moment, still chuckling, then said, "Brrrp brrp, brrp brrrp, brr, '*Hello*'?" He used a high-pitched, squeaky voice for his mother. "Hi Mom, how was your day? '*Oh, you know, same as usual. My knee's been hurting. How about you, son?*' Well you'll never guess where *I've* just been, and who *I've* just been talking to! '*Well don't keep me in suspenders, son. I hope you haven't got yourself into trouble again!*' No, ma'am. I have just been talking to *Melanie Westwood*, in her own home in Bel-Air!"

He laughed long and loud, then drove in silence for a while. When he turned onto Sunset Boulevard he heaved a deep sigh. "I sure hope I don't have to kill her, Mom. I really like Melanie Westwood."

He lapsed into silence and by a roundabout route made his way through Beverly Hills and Mid City to South Broadway, where he left his Toyota at the gas station on the intersection with Slauson Avenue. There he pulled an unused burner from his pocket and dialed a number in France.

* * *

Humberto da Silva was sitting down to have an early dinner. The table at the head of which he sat was large enough to accommodate twenty-four people with comfortable elbow room. The dining room, one of three in the Castèl de Coudrey, had a high ceiling supported on magnificent oak rafters, a fifteenth-century fireplace as big as a Manhattan apartment, and several coats of arms displayed on the walls.

Before him on the table was a classic vichyssoise which his chef, Diat, did exceptionally well, and waiting in the kitchen was a roasted suckling pig with apple sauce, another specialty of his master chef.

He tucked his crisp, white linen napkin into his waistcoat and raised his spoon, and his cell phone rang. He closed his eyes and shook his head.

"*Pourquoi?*" he asked quietly. "*Pourquoi maintenant?*" He picked up the cell. "*Oui?*"

The voice on the other end was quiet, soft, and yet oddly disagreeable.

"Oh, I'm not sure if I have the right number. Did your friend Tom order a steak and fries?"

Humberto grunted. He picked up his heavy, silver

spoon and moved his soup about. "Tell me."

"The steak was delivered suitably deviled and seared, *pour encourager les autres*, as requested, and I just left the fries quivering in the pan. I am pretty sure there will be no need to go for another steak. The fries were appropriately encouraged."

"*Voila*, I am afraid you have the wrong number. I do not know this Tom of whom you speak."

"I apologize, *monsieur*."

"*Bonne soirée*."

He hung up and started in on his soup. So Frazer was dead, and Melanie Westwood had been silenced. He did not, as a rule, favor leaving potential witnesses alive, but this was a rare case. Two high-profile killings so close to each other in space and time would invite too much unwelcome attention. A good scare would do the job, and besides, if she were to speak to anyone, what would she tell, that Frazer Benson was a deluded conspiracy theorist? She would not give them any trouble. And if she did, well, in six months or a year, there would be an unfortunate boating accident, a fall while skiing, or a crash in a tunnel in Paris.

He chuckled as he spooned the last of his cold soup into his mouth and reached for the silver bell. He was ready now for the suckling pig.

TWO

When she stormed through the door into her own living room, the first thing that came into my mind was that she didn't look like any of the characters I had seen her play in the movies. I might have told her so, but she looked pretty mad, so I kept the observation to myself. I would have stood, too, but she sat opposite me before I could get to my feet, and said, "I would like to know just exactly what is going on!"

I raised my eyebrows a little. "That is the story of my life."

"I don't consider this a joking matter, Agent Mason."

"I am sure it's not, and if you tell me what we are talking about exactly, I might be able to tell you just exactly what is going on."

"Well"—she gave her head a rapid shake—"just exactly how many times am I going to have to talk to the FBI? I went to see you voluntarily, you know. Nobody put a gun to my head! Then that awful, creepy special agent yesterday, and n—"

"No."

She blinked a few times. "I *beg* your pardon?"

"There was no special agent yesterday, Miss

Westwood, creepy or otherwise."

"Excuse me, I spoke to him myself. His name was Special Agent Jeremiah Brown." She pointed at me. "He sat right where you are sitting."

I nodded. "I'm sure he did, but he was not from the FBI. Excuse me." I pulled my cell from my pocket and called Lovelock, Nero's assistant.

"Hi, handsome—"

"Good morning. I need you to run a check on one Special Agent Jeremiah Brown. He came to visit Melanie Westwood yesterday and claimed to be from the Bureau. Let the chief know, will you?"

"I'm on it."

I hung up. She was staring at me with her eyes wide and her mouth slightly open. "What the hell!" she said.

"Miss Westwood, I'd like you to tell me all about this Jeremiah Brown, but first of all, I am going to annoy you by asking you to tell me exactly what Frazer Benson said to you at the party." She sighed and seemed to sag. "I know." I added and smiled, "You already told the guys at E. Street, but I bet you have to say your lines a hell of a lot more often than that. Just imagine you're learning lines."

She returned the smile, not entirely without humor. "Funny. Okay, we were at Jack Magnuson's eighty-sixth birthday party. With the number of people who went, I figured I'd be safe from his advances. Believe me, being eighty-six wouldn't stop him. Anyhow, it was fairly late in the night when Frazer approached me. He was another leech—a letch and a leech—he was always either trying to get me to invest my money with him or trying to get into bed with me. Often as not, it was both at the same time. And when you tell him no, he starts trying to impress you with his wealth and influence." She paused. "Well, he used to."

"He said something about a club?"

"Yeah, he said he belonged to some kind of secret society more than a club. It was in France. He told me the members were all like senior politicians, high-ranking officials from the European Union, judges, billionaires. You know the kind of thing."

I smiled. "Yeah, we have a few here."

"Right, Skull and Bones, Bohemian Grove. To name but two."

"Did he say where the club was in France?"

"Yeah, in the Pyrenees, in the area of Occitanie. The village was called Orus, south of Foix, near Val-de-Sos. He said they had a castle, Castèl de Coudrey."

She stopped talking, and I looked up from the notes I was taking. "Something on your mind?"

She took a deep breath. "A couple of things, Agent Mason. You've heard of the Bilderberg Group?"

"Sure."

"Well, he made it sound like that, only more secretive. He said they were rooted in the Hashishim from Persia and controlled international politics, started wars, had people assassinated. It was like the most extreme conspiracy theory sort of stuff." She hesitated a moment. "He hinted heavily that the pandemic was engineered by them as an experiment in social control. And that they were planning something even worse, also involving a virus."

"Did you tell any of this to Jeremiah Brown?"

Her face twisted into a frown. "I started to, but I stopped because he scared me. I got as far as Castèl de

Coudrey and told him no more."

"Okay, good." I scratched my head with my pen. "I want to ask you about him, but before I do, did Benson say any more about this virus? About a lab, its origin, anything at all?"

She shook her head. "No, just that this group, he gave them a name. It was a pretty creepy name, but I thought it was just bullshit. Something about goats. The Brotherhood of the Goat. That was it. This brotherhood had developed a virus that would make the pandemic pale into insignificance."

"That's quite a statement. Did you believe him?"

She shook her head. "Not at the time. He was very drunk. Thankfully, Tom came along and rescued me. Then, next morning, when I heard he had been murdered in that horrible way, and that it looked like a ritual killing"—she shrugged—"I didn't know what to think. So I decided I'd best call you."

I nodded. "That was the right decision. Now, Miss Westwood, what did Jeremiah Brown say to you when he was here?"

She took a deep breath, and her eyes strayed to the window behind me. The light from the garden lay across her face.

"First of all, he wanted to know what Frazer had told me. As I said, I started to tell him, but he just freaked me out, and my instinct told me to stop and tell him no more."

"So you didn't tell him about the virus."

"Right. Then he got really creepy."

"Creepy? Can you be more precise?"

"Well, Agent Mason, I could swear he was

threatening me. He said a man in Frazer's position should not drink or boast. He should be modest, mature, and discreet. Then he said—it's hard to remember because he was so subtle about it—but he said a woman like me who was wealthy and had achieved a lot, and had a lot of people depending on me, had wisdom and intelligence, and that made me discreet."

"He stressed the word discreet, right?"

"Yes, he did. He said"—she squeezed her eyes shut and quoted—"'Indiscretion costs lives, and what is worse, it costs pain. Pain to the indiscreet, to those who love them, and those they love.'"

"That does sound like a threat, Miss Westwood."

She held up a palm to me. "Wait, it's coming back to me, then he said to think of how Frazer had died, he said, 'It's hard for most of us to imagine what he went through, but to a woman with empathy it must be a terrible thing to imagine.' And then he added, 'If only he had been discreet, it might never have happened.'"

I grunted. Then for good measure, I sighed. She said, "The last thing he said before he left was that Frazer was probably just showing off to a beautiful, desirable lady and I should just forget the whole thing."

"Could you describe him?"

Her brow creased. "Thin. Thin legs. Gray hair. Average height. It was odd, his mouth seemed to make a V shape when he smiled, his nose was kind of hooked. And his eyes were a horrible kind of pale blue, almost white."

"It was brave of you to see me. I'm not sure how wise it was. If I had known all this before, I think I might have arranged things differently."

"Yeah, I guess. I thought he was just a weirdo from the FBI. It wasn't till you told me he wasn't FBI..." She trailed off.

"I'm going to put someone on your house, and I'm going to send over a security expert to look the place over and advise you." I gave her my card. "Any problem, or if you think of anything, call me."

I stood while she looked at the card. I asked her, "Do you have a gun?"

She looked up sharply. "No! I don't approve of them."

I arched an eyebrow. "Did Frazer Benson?"

"That's cheap. I suppose you're a member of the NRA!"

"Of course you have the option of dying with your moral integrity intact, but if I were you, I'd take a three-hour drive down I-10 to Ehrenberg in Arizona and get me a good semi-automatic. Then learn to use it. If Jeremiah Brown comes back, he won't be all that interested in your views on gun control."

I left her staring down at my card. Isabel saw me to the door.

I took I-405 to LAX, and on the way, I called Nero.

Lovelock answered. "Hey, ugly."

"Put me through to Caesar, will you? It's urgent."

There was a five-second pause, then, "What?"

"It looks as though we may have stumbled on something big."

"Explain."

"First we need to scramble first class twenty-four-hour security on her house. She needs a security advisor to go see her today. Her life could be seriously at risk."

"Wait."

The line went dead for two minutes. Then he came

back.

"Continue."

"Brotherhood of the Goat, mean anything to you?"

"It brings a few people to mind, but aside from that, not really."

"That's the name of this club. She said what he described was more of a secret society. Membership is powerful politicians, state officials, judges, billionaires. They organize world events, wars, recessions, coups, and the like to favor their investments. You get the idea."

"Yes, so far it sounds just like the Masons, Skull and Bones, Bohemian Grove, and the Bilderberg Group, and a few more I could mention. They don't go around killing members who get drunk and talk at parties. They may have them killed for other reasons, but not that. There'd be none of them left if they did."

"Wouldn't that be a shame. She says he claimed they organized the pandemic, but they are preparing a virus which will make the pandemic pale by comparison."

He went quiet. I was approaching exit fifty-one for Washington Boulevard, and I knew the LAX exit was not far. I said,

"I'm guessing you looked into Frazer's financials."

"Of course. They are still looking."

"I'll keep guessing. You found substantial investments in Hong Kong."

"We did. He is on the boards of Bio-Gen, based in Hong Kong, Hong Kong Financial Holdings, and the Trans-China Investment Corporation."

I nodded. "Okay, I am going to go out on a limb here. One of them, probably Hong Kong Financial

Holdings, invests in Iranian oil."

"Very good, Alex."

"And another one, probably Trans-China Investment, invests heavily in Chinese pharmaceuticals. Am I way off?"

"No, you are absolutely right. Of course, they invest more widely, but those are significant investments."

"What about Bio-Gen? What do they do?"

"On the face of it, they are an IT research and development company."

I nodded. "Sir, we have a very big problem on our hands."

"I am aware."

"I need to go to France."

"Before you do that, come back to DC. We'll discuss what steps are to be taken."

I came off at exit forty-six for LAX and headed for the company jet.

It was a little less than four hours, and with the time difference, it was almost nine p.m. by the time I disembarked.

In the parking lot, in the fading light of the dusk, I saw a man in a dark suit standing beside my car as I approached. I pressed the button on my key fob, and the trunk clunked open. He stepped forward.

"Mr. Mason?"

"That depends. Who are you?"

"My name is Bob, Mr. Nero's driver. He is waiting for you in his car." He gestured to a vintage Rolls parked down the line. "If you'll follow me."

I followed him, aware of my P226 heavy under my arm, and shifted my bag to my left hand. The car was a beauty, a 1967 cream Phantom V. He had obviously made adjustments because as we approached, the rear window slid down electronically, and he peered out at me.

"Give Bob your bag and the key to your vehicle. I assume you haven't eaten. We'll dine and talk."

I gave Bob the items in question and climbed in the back. I saw he had another Bob behind the wheel. "How many Bobs have you got?"

The car pulled away as silently as a ghost and we moved toward the 14th Street Bridge.

"You will go to France," he said. "But we need to think carefully. One mistake, Alex, one, however simple, could have consequences that are incalculable." He went silent, but I knew better than to say anything. He raised a finger. "Every successful operation depends on sufficient good intelligence." He turned to look at me. "And we have exactly none. We have just enough intelligence to goad us into urgent action, but nowhere near enough to make that action effective."

I nodded. It seemed a fair assessment.

"Therefore, we must arrange to acquire intelligence simultaneously while we take action."

"How do we do that?"

"Shut up, Alex." We were moving over the dark water. "You need to become a member of the Brotherhood of the Goat. Now here we must proceed with care. Note the sacrificial nature of Frazer Benson's execution and the reference to the goat in the name of the society. So we must be alert to the possibility that there is some kind of mystical element or angle to this brotherhood."

"Yes, I had—"

"Don't speak. The goat suggests a Mediterranean or

Middle Eastern root. Azazel is a fallen angel mentioned in the Torah, one of those responsible for introducing humans to the forbidden knowledge. He is extremely ancient. A goat was traditionally sent to him at Yom Kippur, bearing the sins of the Jewish people. You may know that a similar tradition existed in Syria relating to the king's marriage. We have Pan—the root of our word panic, for he struck terror into people's hearts and drove them to madness—an amoral god renowned for his sexual prowess and his lust. We have also the Baphomet from the times of the Crusades which drew on a rich heritage of goat-related mythology and was absorbed into black magic and witchcraft." He glanced at me. "In essence, the goat in Eastern and Middle Eastern tradition represents fertility and sexual prowess, madness, and more recently, the blurring of the boundaries between good and evil." He raised his finger again. "These may be the foundations of the Brotherhood's philosophy."

I rubbed my face. "This is a lot to take in. I need a drink."

"You have heard of Hassan-i-Sabbah?"

"Uh, he rings a bell."

"He founded the Hashishim in 1090, in Persia, at the Alamut Castle. The Hashishim were the Order of Assassins, a Nizari Isma'ili order, a sect of Shia Islam. But despite being a Muslim, Hassan was also fascinated by philosophy and mysticism, and recent writings that have been found in Persia suggest that he may have been in a cult that venerated Azazel, whose earliest incarnation is as the Babylonian god Ea, and before that the Sumerian god Enki, the horned goat."

"This would be fascinating," I said weakly, feeling a headache coming on.

"The least you need to know right now," he said as we pulled up at the corner of 6th and Pennsylvania, outside the Capital Grill, "is that this Brotherhood may well be steeped in goat worship dating back to the tenth century, and perhaps to early Sumerian mysticism."

"Great. Don't you just love it when that happens?"

We climbed out, and I followed him toward the comfort of good steak, good wine, and whiskey.

THREE

ortified with a large Bushmills straight up, I opted for pan-fried calamari with hot cherry peppers followed by sliced filet mignon with cipollini onions, wild mushrooms and fig essence, while Nero opted for a jumbo lump crab cocktail followed by a tomahawk veal chop with sage butter, Marsala jus and crispy prosciutto. Nero ordered a Vin Santo Riserva from 2016 for the crab and the calamari and a big, beefy Barolo Cannubi from 2017 for the steak. So by the time we were done ordering, I was feeling strong enough to take another look at the goat.

I took a generous sip of whiskey and said, "So let me see if I have a handle on this." Nero took a sip of his martini and leaned back to watch me. I went on, "The apparent ritual nature of the murder, and the reference to the goat in their name, suggests to you that this club may be into some dark kind of mysticism."

"He was nailed to the floor, with his arms in a cross and his legs akimbo, to form a pentagram, with his head aligned with the east and his groin to the west. A circle had been drawn around him. He had been castrated, disemboweled, and two holes had been drilled into his skull where the goat's horns would be. Finally, his heart was removed. Thankfully, we must assume by that time he was already dead."

"So if you are right, which you always are, these things that were done to him have some kind of meaning."

"He is nailed to the floor. This signifies the imprisonment of the human soul, bound to the Earth and deprived of its power. That is to say, the human will fettered by the basic rules of physics."

"Okay."

"The pentagram has long been a symbol in Western and Eastern mysticism. It symbolizes the five senses which limit and shape our knowledge and understanding, the five elements, and the source of all temporal power. Shifted forty-five degrees, the pentagram becomes a representation of the goat's head, with horns, beard, and ears."

He took a sip of his drink.

"His alignment east to west relates to the prison of time, where the sun rises and sets. None of us, Alex, can ever escape from now, either to the past or to the future, however much we may wish to, and yet, according to the mystics, he who is able actually to *be* in the now may find freedom."

I grunted and sipped my whiskey.

"He was castrated, removing his ability not only to give life, but to extend his own genetic existence. He was disemboweled, depriving him of the ability to benefit from the world's abundance, and his heart was removed, depriving him of the ability to love or enjoy love. Finally, openings were made for his demonic horns to grow, allowing him to be reborn—to re-become—as a daemon."

"Okay, so it was a ritual murder—"

"Execution."

"All right, it was a ritual execution. So we can take the next step, then, and say that the name of the cult gives us a clue as to the nature of their..." I hesitated.

"Philosophy—"

I nodded. "The philosophy of the cult. Sure, seen like that, it makes perfect sense."

"Thank you." He said it with just a hint of sarcasm. "Do you wish to continue?"

"Just a bit. So we can probably assume that if this cult is recruiting high achievers, it's not based on the kind of pseudo-kabalistic ritualism you can dig up on Google. Hence"—I gestured at him—"the goat stuff you told me about in the car."

"The goat," he said, "was in all probability the first animal to be domesticated after the beginning of the interglacial period, some ten thousand years ago. Though in the light of Gobekli Tepe, it may have been before that. So its connection with ritual goes back to the earliest times of our civilization. The earliest gods we know of, those of Sumeria, elevated the goat to the status of Enki, the bringer of teaching and knowledge to humanity. This role later became corrupted as the myths moved from Sumeria and Babylon into Palestine, and Enki became equated with Lucifer and Satan, who induced human woman to eat from the forbidden fruit of the tree of knowledge. It is all tied up with the fallen angels who mated with human women and started teaching humans how to plow and build cities."

"How does all that help us?"

"It gives us a little insight into their thinking. I myself am not a religious man, Alex, and I have no wish to know whether you are. However, there is a school of religious thought that claims we are the victims of a great deception. That Lucifer was the good guy, so to speak, and the bad guys were Elohim. Lucifer brought us learning and civilization, and Elohim tried to crush us and keep us in ignorance. When mankind took Lucifer's teachings, Elohim punished us by bringing about the Great Flood and all but wiping out humanity."

I sat back to allow the waiter space to deliver the calamari and the crab. Meanwhile another waiter brought an ice bucket with the wine, poured some for Nero to try and watched him sniff and sip. Nero grunted and nodded. The waiter poured and went away.

I said,

"Elohim?"

"Yes, the god of the Old Testament," he said and stuffed his mouth full of crab, chewed, grunted again, swallowed, and sipped. "Superb, very good, indeed. The Christian god only becomes Jehovah after he speaks to Moses in the form of a burning bush, Alex. Having given Moses his instructions, Moses asks him, 'Whom shall I say has told me this?' and God answers, 'Tell them I am who I am. Thus shall you say to the children of El that Ehyeh has sent you.' Ehyeh means 'I am' in Hebrew. Moses tells God he doesn't think they will understand, so God says, 'Thus shall you say to the people of Israel, Yahweh, Elohim of your fathers, has sent you.' Yahweh translates somewhat simplistically as 'He is,' with a nuance of 'and always will be.'"

"So before the burning bush, Jehovah was Elohim."

"It would seem so, though it is odd that Elohim is plural and actually means gods, or powerful ones."

I ate calamari and drank wine.

"Sir, this obviously makes a lot of sense to you."

"Alex, if the signs are correct, we may be facing a religious fanatic who is fixated on the acquisition of knowledge to be used ruthlessly for the accruing of power. What he did—or had done—to Frazer Benson will give us a measure of the extremes to which he is prepared to go."

I smiled blandly. "Well, for heaven's sake, why didn't you say so? Do we have any idea who this man might be?"

"Yes. He is a Frenchman of Portuguese extraction, by the name of Humberto da Silva. He is a Commissioner at the European Commission, at the head of Directorate General 32, trade, he has three PhDs in philosophy, psychology, and economics, and he has very quietly become a billionaire listed in the Forbes One Hundred."

"Boy, how did you find him?"

He arched an eyebrow at me as he sipped his wine. "Archie, I inquired who owned Castèl de Coudrey."

"That would do it."

We finished our starters in silence while I turned over everything he had told me.

They took away our plates and brought the Barolo for Nero to try. He gave it his approval, and when our steaks had been served, he told me, "The forensic economy department is still at work on Frazer Benson's finances, and they have started on Humberto da Silva's, so what I am going to tell you is preliminary. However, it seems that both men sat on the boards of Hong Kong Financial Holdings and the Trans-China Investment Corporation, amongst others. You will recall that Hong Kong Financial Holdings invests in Iranian oil."

"I remember." I told him that through a mouth full of filet mignon with fig essence. He took a moment to cut into his veal chop, and before popping a slice into his mouth he said, "We traced his parents. His father was Lord Chudleigh, a minor English aristocrat from Devon. But his mother was Portuguese on her father's side, but Persian on her mother's side."

"Persian?" I frowned as I drank.

"She came from a rich, aristocratic family who fled to Portugal when the Ayatollahs came to power at the beginning of 1979. Humberto, it seems, has chosen his mother's name and does not often use his father's title."

"Huh!"

"Indeed."

"So how did he become French?"

"He moved to France to read for his doctorate in Cartesian philosophy. He stayed and became naturalized. Some ten years later, now in his mid forties, he bought the Castèl de Coudrey, which, I should mention, was built in the late twelfth century by Sir Hugh de Coudrey, Baron of Godneston, a Knight Templar whose son, Lacklan, would join Richard Coeur de Lion on the Third Crusade. The Templars, of course, worshipped the Baphomet."

"The image of the goat in the pentagram."

"Correct."

I finished my filet mignon in silence and drained my glass of Barolo. When I had it refilled and had sat back in my chair, I said, "Okay, you have persuaded me that the Brotherhood has a sinister and dangerous fetish about goats and a very dangerous ideological approach to gathering intelligence to accrue power. You have also convinced me—and this has a more immediate bearing on our discussion—that whatever the Brotherhood is doing, it involves Iran as well as China."

He signaled the waiter while he asked me, "Why has that a more immediate bearing?"

"Because if this bunch of very powerful crazies is manufacturing a virus, that has to be of real interest to Israel."

"Israel is not part of the Five Eyes, Alex. We can't share intelligence with them without going through channels."

"So go through channels, meantime let me contact Captain Gallin. I won't tell her anything she doesn't know already."

He considered my face for a long moment, then looked down at his plate.

"What you have just said, Alex, makes absolutely no sense. However, provided you do not reveal any confidential information to her, contact her. I shall talk to her father, in London. Ah—"

This last was directed at the waiter, who had appeared at the table. He ordered two twenty-one-year-old Bushmills, no ice, to be served in cognac glasses, two espresso coffees, and a board of mature sheep's cheese.

"What I shall want from you, Alex, is that you go to France. We have access to a small but rather exquisite vineyard just outside Boussenac, a mere twenty miles or so from the castle. You shall be the new owner."

"A vineyard in the mountains?"

"Yes, we grow the Manseng grape there, which thrives in the mountains. It has a low yield but produces an exquisite, aromatic fresh wine. You'll enjoy it. Your purpose will be to engage the interest of this Humberto da Silva. It may help that he is known as something of a gourmet. You might try and get him to take an interest in your vineyard."

"When? I'm going to need time to bone up on this Manseng grape and your Baphomets."

"Not yet." He picked up his whiskey and didn't so much sniff it as inhale it. "You have a few days."

He dropped me at my house on Adam Street, and I watched his taillights disappear into the night. I let myself in, and after fending off an ambush by Manny Pacquiao, my cat, I poured myself a small nightcap of twenty-one-year-old Bushmills, dropped into an armchair in my drawing room, and stared at the black glass between my open drapes.

Goats, Baphomets, ritual murder, and vineyards, not to mention Sumerian gods and Iranian viruses. I shook my head at Manny and told him, "Nuts," sipped my whiskey, and called Gallin. It rang a few times before her sleepy voice said, "What the hell, Mason! It's five in the morning!"

"Only where you are, Gallin. There are twenty-three other time zones in this world."

"What the hell are you talking about?" You could tell from her voice that she had her face screwed up.

"Are you alone?"

"*What?*"

"Are-you-a-lone? I need to talk to you."

"Yes! Of course I'm alone!"

I smiled to myself but didn't let it show in my voice. "I need you to be my wife."

There was the sound of her moving, probably sitting up. "Mason, are you drunk?"

"Let me see, I have had a *very* long day, got off the plane from Los Angeles and was driven straight to the

Capital Grill, where I had half a bottle of white, half a bottle of red and two large Bushmills. I am now on my third. Nope, not drunk."

"So proposing marriage to me is a *sober* terrible life choice?"

"You heard about Frazer Benson?"

The change in her voice was subtle. It told me she knew I was telling her something important. "Yeah. Oh, Los Angeles. That's why you were in LA?"

"I don't know how much you got over on your side of the pond. Here the media were saying it was a ritual execution."

"That's what they're saying here. Do you believe it?" She was wide awake now.

I used my foot to pull over a burgundy leather pouf and crossed my ankles on it.

"Yeah, it certainly seems likely, from the details. Man, that guy's investments were wild. He had made it into the billionaires' club in the last couple of years."

"Yeah?"

"Yup, investments in China"—I paused for effect —"Iran, artificial intelligence research, petrochemicals, vaccines..." I trailed off.

"Interesting bloke."

"You can say that again. Hey, listen, real reason I'm calling. I have acquired a vineyard in the Pyrenees."

"Really." There was no interrogative intonation. It was just a flat, dry comment.

"Yeah, the grapes are Manseng. I'm sure you're familiar with them. Low yield but highly aromatic and fresh. I would like you to come there with me as my wife."

She didn't answer for a long moment. Then she

said, "There was a song. How did it go? *Je avais un residence, Je habiter la, in the sarf du France. Voulez vous, partir with me?* And *rester la* with me in France."

By the time she'd finished, she was laughing. I let her finish and told her, "I'm serious."

"I dunno, Mason. I've always thought of you as a friend. Waking up, seeing your head on the pillow next to mine... Would you still respect me? Do you snore? So many questions."

"My dad is going to talk to your dad. Meantime, hop on a plane, come to DC, we'll discuss it."

"Can we have a white wedding?"

"We can have it whatever color you like, except pink or rainbow."

"I'll talk to Daddy over breakfast. If he says it's okay, you can meet me at the airport. You keep changing cars. What have you got now?"

"A twenty-three-year-old Jag S-Type. V8, three hundred and eighty-nine horses."

"Nice, not crazy, but nice. Maybe it's time you settled and got married."

"It's what I'm telling you."

"I need another hour's sleep. I'll call you after breakfast with Daddy."

"Sleep tight."

"And you stop boozing and go to bed."

I hung up and sat staring at the black glass again.

FOUR

As Gallin stood, wrapped in a towel, with water dripping over her face from her wet hair, telling her father over the phone that she was on her way to have breakfast with him, six hundred miles to the south, Humberto da Silva was having breakfast on a terrace overlooking his Italian gardens. He was in a green Harris tweed with a silk cravat, and by his side was Dr. Hussein Sasani. The table was set with a white linen cloth. The coffee pot, the milk jug, the sugar bowl, and the butter dish were all fifteenth-century silver. They were eating brioche and croissants, Dr. Sasani with a silver knife, also from the fifteenth century, Humberto with his large hands. He ripped and buttered and stuffed with energy and appetite.

"So, Doctor," he said with his mouth full, "what progress have you got to report to me?"

The doctor nodded, swallowed, and sipped. "We are making progress, my lord, but we are at a very delicate stage. The stage of *transmission*. Because we want"—he paused to arrange the butter dish, the milk jug, and the basket of croissants in a semicircle, and then approached with his fingers, walking like legs—"when this individual approaches, we want him to *transmit* to the butter dish and to the milk jug, perhaps the coffee pot, but we *do not* want him to transmit to the basket of croissants. This is a different category, and we want to protect this category. But here is the problem."

He sat back and dabbed his mouth with his white napkin.

"Here is the problem. Just because the category is different, it does not mean the receptors are different. If I can make a comparison which is quite relevant, COVID-19 was *indiscriminate*. It doesn't care if you are Chinese, Black, American, man, or woman. Because all of the receptors are the same." He made elaborate gestures toward his body with his hands. *"The processes by which the virus is assimilated and integrated are the same.* So what we are doing now is showing, teaching the virus how to recognize a target, and how to recognize one who is not a target."

"Good." Humberto helped them both to coffee. "How are you doing this, Doctor?"

"We are using two methods in combination with each other. We are confident we have it right now and this is going to work. First, we are writing a program in a piece of protein with a photon laser. I m talking about a piece of protein too small to see with the naked eye."

"Of course."

"Then, we are inserting this protein into the virus so that it is interfacing with the genetic material. Now, after this, we are subjecting it to *one million situations*, virtually, one thousand situations in a minute, positive, negative, yes, no, good result bad result. For sixteen hours, the virus is learning what is a target and what is not a target."

"You insert the viruses in a chamber and the computer feeds these, uh, *situations* you call them, into the viruses, who use the program you have written into the protein to learn from this positive and negative situations."

"That is exactly, precisely it, my lord."

"When will you know if it has worked? Time is of the essence, Doctor. Our hour approaches."

"We need sixteen hours for the *bombardment* to end, and then we need some days to test the responses of the virus. I hope that within a week we will have the virus ready for deployment."

Humberto smiled, then he chuckled. "That is very exciting, Dr. Sasani. That is very exciting indeed. We may both soon see our dreams become reality."

"Allahu Akbar!"

Nothing changed in Humberto's face. The smile remained, the curve of his lips, the crease of his eyes. Yet all the warmth and humor seemed to drain from his expression.

"Indeed," he said, "may the light shine upon us all." The doctor inclined his head in acknowledgement. Humberto dabbed his lips. "Well, Doctor, I must not keep you selfishly for my own pleasure. I am sure you must be anxious to get back to work. We shall speak again in sixteen hours, I hope."

Dr. Hussein Sasami bowed his head again, rose, bowed from the waist, and left for his laboratory. Humberto watched him leave with a mixture of amusement and contempt. There was no doubt in his mind that Sasani represented a lower species within the human race, that was indeed the bulk of the human race. They were the fruit of the seeds sown long ago, by his own ancestors. There was no doubt in his mind about this.

When Sasani called him "my lord," as an increasing number of people did, the Iranian believed the title derived from Humberto's English aristocratic rank. But he, Humberto, knew the true reason for the title. The title had come to him from the great ones in the sky, because he had awakened to his own true nature. He *was* a Lord! And soon, the whole world would know it.

* * *

In Hong Kong, Mike Chen, the CEO of Bio-Gen, received a phone call. The screen of his telephone told him it was Humberto da Silva, calling from France. So he took his time. He picked up the phone, eased his huge, black leather chair away from his vast, black carbon fiber desk, and walked to the plate-glass wall that overlooked the harbor. Once there, he answered. It was three p.m., so it must be nine a.m. in France.

"Good morning, Humberto. I gather you have finished breakfast. If I remember correctly, you break your fast at eight."

"Good morning, Mike. I breakfasted with Dr. Hussein Sasami this morning."

"Is he making progress?"

"He tells me that in sixteen hours he will be ready for final testing. It is probably time for you to go to New York."

"Is he bullshitting or will he deliver?"

"He has not failed me yet, Mike. He is good at what he does."

"He is not Persian, you know. He is an Iranian monkey."

"Are you questioning my objectivity, Mike? Do I

41

need to remind you who is running this show?"

Mike Chen smiled down at the churning, bustling anthill beneath him. "No, Lord Chudleigh of Devon. I know very well who is in charge of the operation."

Humberto's voice came cold and dangerous. "Do not make a mistake, Mike. We are at the threshold. Don't fuck it up now."

"I won't, Humberto. I will be on the next flight to New York. Relax."

He hung up and spoke aloud, still gazing out at the city.

"May Ling, get me on the next flight to New York. Call home and get Geoffrey to pack me a bag and pick me up at the office in time for the flight."

The voice that answered came from a speaker on his desk. It said, "Yes, Mr. Chen, right away."

* * *

On Bordeaux Drive, in Lakewood, San Francisco, it was midnight. Sean Hagin, the senior partner in Hagin da Silva Biotech, was working late. Information technology, he had noticed in the past year or two, was changing. It was a slow and subtle change that would not be obvious to most. But he had his connections, connections that were out, ahead of the cutting edge, and he was aware that IT was moving on the one hand away from the silicon chip and toward the biochip and artificial intelligence, and on the other hand toward space. The next hundred years, he was sure, would see biological AI computers in space.

He only wished he could be there to see it.

Before him on his desk were the plans and costings

for a lab. At the moment, this was a speculative project, but that had been his brief: to prepare a speculative project which could be implemented at a moment's notice. Because this lab would be conducting research and development into biochips—on the moon, funded by Chinese financiers.

The phone rang, and he put it to his ear.

"Hagin."

"Sean, how are things developing at your end?"

"Oh, Mr. da Silva, I'm just here burning the midnight oil. We're almost there. We just need to finish a few details—"

"Good, good. Excellent. Sean, forgive me for interrupting. I am sure you are keen to wrap up for the night, and I must get to work. Look here, the good doctor informs me that our product is all but finished. In sixteen hours, a little less now, he is confident he can start the final tests."

Sean's voice, when he answered, was husky with suppressed excitement.

"That is wonderful news."

"So I think it is probably time for you to book a flight to London. Get some sleep and depart tomorrow morning."

"Yes, Mr. da Silva. I will do that straight away."

"Good, good. Excellent."

He hung up and sat gazing at the plans before him, and after a moment he began to weep from sheer joy.

FIVE

She came through arrivals looking like a million bucks on legs. She was in boot-cut Levis, a khaki shirt, and what looked like Spanish riding boots. But if she'd been in a satin evening gown with a neckline to her belly button and a slash up to her right hip, she couldn't have looked any better than she did right then. She had a brown pigskin bag slung over her shoulder, and I knew that was all her baggage.

She walked up to me, where I was standing, with a particular kind of smile on her face. I couldn't place it, but I knew it was particular. I said, "Can I carry your books?"

"If I can ride in your car."

"I think we have a deal." I reached for her bag and took it. "But you know you're going to have to marry me."

We headed for the parking lot, pushing through the crowds. She took my arm and asked, "Do I get a white picket fence?"

"Nope, but you do get a vineyard in the foothills of the Pyrenees."

She glanced at me from under an arched eyebrow. "You're serious."

"I am. How much has your dad told you?"

"Not much. He said Nero had called him and told

him there were things he couldn't tell him. My dad does a pretty good impression of Nero, did I ever tell you that?"

"No."

"When he is not in his official capacity, he is a really funny guy. We should have dinner one day. He'll make you laugh. Anyhow, we were having breakfast, and he said, 'Nero called me. I picked up the phone, 'Hello, Gabriel Gallin speaking,' and he says, straight off, no hello no nothing, he says, 'There are things I cannot tell you, Gabriel.'"

We had arrived at the Burgundy Beast. I popped the trunk and slung her bag in. "That sounds like Nero. Why waste time on courtesy?"

"That is a beautiful car."

"They tell me it will be a classic."

"Can I drive it?"

"You can, but you mayn't." I opened the driver's door and spoke across the roof. "Right now, you finish telling me about your dad, and then you listen to what I have to tell you about our future married life together."

I climbed in and closed the door. She got in beside me. I turned the key and made the big V8 snarl. She slammed her door harder than was necessary.

"You know what the Spanish say?"

"Olé?"

"They say, '*Tu madre es una santa, pero tu eres un hijo de la gran puta!*'"

I cruised out of the lot, regarding her with an arched eyebrow. "I didn't know you spoke Spanish. What does it mean?"

"Your mother is a saint, but you are a son of the great whore."

"Wow. That's intense. You have to eat a lot of garlic to come up with something like that. So you were telling me about your dad."

We joined I-395 and crossed into DC over the water. She watched that happen though her window for a moment, then said, "Yeah, so Nero told my dad pretty much what you had told me, but with more gory details." She frowned at me a moment. "They really put Benson through it."

I nodded. "He must have really upset somebody with some very particular ideas about punishment."

"Yeah. I guess. Anyhow, so Nero told him they were in a pretty absurd situation because all the information he had was available in the public domain, but when you put it all together as an investigation, it became classified. 'So, Gabriel, my dear friend, though this may be of significant consequence to Israel, I cannot share it with you until it has been cleared though the appropriate channels.'"

"That's good. You sound like him."

"Then he asked after me and said that perhaps I needed a holiday after the strain of recent events in Spain. Did my dad think it would be a good idea for me to come and spend a couple of weeks with you. Like that would ease the strain."

"Your father obviously thought it would."

"Yeah, so right now, half of the London field office of the Mossad is looking into Frazer Benson's business dealings and relationships. They'll get back to me as and when they turn up anything of relevance. I'm hoping you will fill me in before that."

We passed the Jefferson Memorial on 14th Street

and headed north.

"Some men," I said, "might fall into the trap of pillow talk, Gallin, but I am not one of them."

"Keep dreaming, asshole. You asked for me, remember? What's this about?"

I nodded. "Goats."

She shrugged and spread her hands. "Goats…"

"There is a man in France, whose mother was Persian—"

"Not Iranian."

"Persian, and aristocratic. His father was English and minor aristocratic. He has bought himself a castle in the Pyrenees which glories in the name Castèl Coudrey. Coudrey Castle was built by an English nobleman in the thirteenth century. He was a Templar who accompanied Richard *Coeur de Lion*"—as we were being all multilingual, I pronounced it the French way—"on the Third Crusade and, so I am told by Nero, worshiped the Baphomet."

"The goat in the pentagram."

"You got it."

"And who is this man who bought this castle?"

"His name is Humberto da Silva."

"That's a Portuguese name. It is neither Persian nor English. It's Portuguese."

"Yeah, I know. It's his mother's dad's name, and it gets kind of Freudian. But that is his name. And he is the head or leader or whatever they are called, Grand Master, of a society called The Brotherhood of the Goat."

She looked away, out of the window at the Ronald Reagan Building as it slid by and muttered, "*Hob rachmones!*"

"Who?"

She turned to look at me. "Have pity. It's like saying, Jesus. Jesus! *Hob rachmones!*" She pulled her phone from her pocket and made a call. She talked for about five minutes in what I assumed was Hebrew and then hung up.

I smiled at her. "Dad okay?"

"Yeah, he says hi. So what's the plan?"

"Lunch at my place. Then I think we go shopping and get you some luggage. After that, we can plan our wedding."

"That sounds like fun...darling. Weren't you married before once? Didn't she commit suicide?"

"No." She looked surprised. I said, "I strangled her for an excess of sass."

We got home and made lunch. I subjected her to diced filet of salmon stir-fried with diced ginger root, garlic, onions, and tender green beans on brown rice seasoned with tamari. While I made that, she sat and watched me, drinking a beer as Manny Pacquiao kneaded her leg shamelessly before curling up and sleeping on her lap. Cats will always get away with things that would get any man thrown in jail. If you don't believe me, ask Fat Freddy.

We sat at the barbeque table in the backyard and ate to the sound of the birds and the bees making free with the roses.

I told her, "Nero has a vineyard just outside Boussenac. Boussenac is a village just twenty miles from Coudrey Castle. We are going to arrive there as the new owners, Arthur and Anne Beaumont of San Francisco. We made our money developing agro-software."

"Agro-what?"

"Software designed to assist in agriculture, and we have bought this vineyard which grows the rare and aromatic Manseng grape and we plan to make sweet, dessert wines from it, but also to explore the possibilities of oak aged table wines."

She elevated her eyebrows and nodded. "Could be fun. I see a future for us after all."

"Good to know. The downside is that we have to explore and frequent the gourmet restaurants of the area, as far north as Perpignan and Foix."

"Darn that bad luck!"

"Apparently Mr. da Silva is a gourmet, and we want to pal up with him and start to share our fascination with the occult, and the occult history of the area, particularly its connection with the Templars."

"Gotcha. We hope that once we are pals, he will invite us to one of his ritual executions, or summoning the devil of a Sunday morning."

"Something like that, but more likely—you may not know this, but I have recently become a billionaire—we try to lure him into inviting us to invest in his project."

"Which is…?"

I hesitated. "This is something your pals at the Mossad are busy trying to find out as we speak, right?"

She sighed. "I could get violent, Mason. I warn you I am skilled at interrogation. Don't make me come over there."

"Fancy your chances?"

For just a moment, it almost happened. For just a moment, we shared—and we knew we shared—the crazy image of wrestling and somehow winding up on the sofa in the living room. But she burst out laughing, and so did

I.

"Come on, Mason! In the next hour they're going to phone me and tell me. Or Nero is going to call you and tell you it's been cleared."

"I have no idea what you are talking about, young lady." I stood and advanced on her to take her empty bowl. "You want some dates and coffee? You have to be careful with dates, did you know that?"

"Yeah. That's why I never date."

"You can get hepatitis from dates. And it can spread like..." I paused and turned to stare at her, and said with great deliberation, "A virus."

"Shit."

"No dates. Especially from Iran."

"Oh, man!"

I went into the kitchen, and she followed. She leaned on the jamb while I set about making coffee.

"So this guy"—she paused—"has a date farm in Iran."

"Apparently. It's possible. I honestly know as much as you will know when they send you the file they are putting together now. And most of what we know, we don't actually *know*. It is more a case of speculation and conjecture that Nero has tolerated because of the potentially disastrous consequences of neglecting it if that conjecture turns out to be right."

"Right, so the job is in fact to find out."

"Yeah, partly."

"Partly, but?"

"It depends what we find out."

"And if we find out the dates are infected?"

"Worst case scenario, the dates are infected, and

neither you nor I can consult with higher authority, we take whatever steps are necessary to neutralize the dates."

She grinned. "We like that option, right?"

"Best case scenario, we contact your boss or mine and call in an air strike or three."

She raised a hand. "Third option. We *try*, really hard, to contact a higher authority, but we can't, so we go all Viking on their ass, then we discover we *can* contact *my* boss, and call in some heavy duty air strikes."

The coffee pot gurgled. I poured her a cup of rich, black brew and said, "See? That's why I like you so much. You are so easy to please."

We spent the afternoon shopping for the kind of clothes and accessories that were appropriate to educated middle class vine-huggers who have become billionaires overnight.

In the evening, we had sirloin steak and French fries with a bottle of Muga *gran reserva* to make up for what I had made her eat at lunch, and spent the evening, until two a.m. reading up on the Manseng grape and the complexities of agro-software.

We got four hours' sleep, me in my bed and Gallin in the guest room with a very smug-looking Manny Pacquiao, and at six a.m. we rose, me to make breakfast and Gallin to pack our cases. We showered and dressed, and at nine a.m., we boarded the company Bombardier headed for our brand-new chateau in the French Pyrenees. I sank into the soft, cream leather seat at the high-polish walnut table, and Gallin settled opposite me in a cream Armani suit that had cost her as much as my classic Jag. Her hair was done in a casual bun at the back of her neck, and she had real diamonds hanging from her ears on long chains beside her neck.

"You look good," I told her.

"You don't look half bad yourself, Mr. Beaumont."

"We're married," I told her.

"Yup."

"That's going to take some getting used to."

She pulled a Rex Stout paperback from her jacket pocket and smiled at it with a touch of mischief at the corner of her mouth. "It might be easier than we think," she said, winked at me, and opened the book.

SIX

We landed at Les Pujols airport, just east of Saint-Jean-du-Falga. Nero had arranged for Ferrer, the chateau manager, to meet us in the Range Rover. He spoke Occitan followed by passable French, and English that in the hands of the wrong people could cause an international incident.

He was gnarled and weather-beaten and had a congenital Gauloise that grew out of his lower lip. He didn't wear a beret, but he did have a shapeless hat, bowed legs, and hands like the roots from an oak tree. He smiled a lot, and when he spoke, he seemed to be gargling nicotine. I couldn't find a single thing to dislike about the guy. In fact, I decided that if humanity was ever saved from its near-inevitable doom, it would be thanks to people like Ferrer.

He laughed as he grabbed our cases and slung them in the trunk. Between case and case, he would put his two index fingers together side by side and rasp, "*Maridèn, eh? Maridèn! Òsca! Òsca!*"

I gathered he thought it was great we were married, so I grinned, gave him the thumbs up, and climbed in the back.

It was only about thirty miles to the chateau,

but at least half of it was through mountains, and a good portion of that was along poor roads that wound endlessly through dense forest. Ferrer didn't seem to be in any kind of a hurry, either, and the drive that would probably have taken Gallin about half an hour wound up taking us slightly more than an hour.

When we finally pulled in through the big iron gates and cruised down the gravel drive, Gallin muttered, "Man, if this is Nero's, he is pulling down some kind of money."

The house was three stories high, plus a gabled roof which I imagined contained a sizeable attic. It was triangular and had a tower shaped like a witch's hat at each of its three corners. It was painted salmon pink with white windows and white shutters, and framing the house on all sides were well-tended gardens, broad lawns, and beyond them, dense woodland.

Ferrer pulled up at the bottom of a shallow flight of semi-circular steps that led up to a classic French gable-arched door. He swung down from the cab and opened the door for Gallin. As she stepped down, he gestured to the house and rasped, "*Benvengut, dòna!*"

He carried our cases up and introduced us to a woman who was like a female version of him. He called her "*Mon Molher,*" which I took to mean "my woman," or "my wife."

She took us to our room, which was about the size of an apartment in DC. It had two arched windows overlooking the woodland and, in the distance, acres of vineyards. It also had a very large four-poster bed which was probably twice as old as the United States.

She didn't stop talking all the while, though what she was saying was a mystery. Finally, she backed out of the room, bobbing and grinning, still talking. Gallin watched her, grinned back, gave her a hug, and finally she left.

We showered and changed, and that afternoon a young man with floppy hair and a blue blazer turned up while we were exploring the ground floor. We had found the dining room and the drawing room, and a large terrace overlooking an Italian garden at the back, when Ferrer showed the guy with the floppy hair where we were.

"Mr. and Mrs. Beaumont? I am Mylan Visage, I manage the estate and the vineyard. Well"—he shrugged and spread his hands—"I have managed it until now, under the previous owner. I hope you will continue to use my services."

We told him we would, and after a brief conversation, he offered to show us the study, the ballroom, the gym, and the library. It was in the library, which had twelve-foot French doors out onto the terrace, that I asked him, "I've heard there is someone here who might be interested in our project to make table wines from our grapes."

He looked surprised. "Really? Who is he?"

"Oh." I snapped my fingers several times. "He has a Portuguese name. Darling?"

She was staring up at the rows of books fifteen feet above her head, nestled in the deep mahogany shelves. I put my arm around her shoulders, and she hooked her thumb in my belt with a small gurgle.

"Da Silva, Humberto da Silva," she said, watching Mylan's face. "He owns Castèl Coudrey, near Sentenac and a village called Orus. Do you know it?"

"*Mais oui!* But yes, of course. But I had no idea."

"That's what I heard on the grapevine!" I winked at Gallin. "Get it?" We all made the effort to laugh. Then I asked him, "So how would I go about getting in touch with him? I heard he is something of a gourmet. Maybe you could give us a list of the best restaurants in the area and we'll try to bump into him."

He nodded vigorously. "Naturally. Of course. And let me make enquiries. I am sure I know somebody who knows him. I can, uh, send the word."

After that he took us in the Range Rover to visit the vineyard and gave us a detailed, and I have to say informative, introduction to the Manseng grape itself, why it was different, and why it was rare as a table wine. After that, he showed us the presses and explained the whole process of pressing, fermenting and aging in oak casks, followed by the bottling and further maturing.

Beside the press was a stone building that resembled some kind of cathedral. Within it, there were huge barrels stacked on top of each other in pyramids, each dated in chalk with brief comments beside the date. Here we sampled the wine, and I had to admit it was pretty good.

"The previous owner," he told us, "was very interested in developing this table wine. I was very surprised when I heard he had sold the chateau. He was passionate. Him..."—he paused, gazing out at the sunlit vines—"him and also his wife."

I stared at him, took a hefty pull on my wine, stared at Gallin, who was frowning, and said, "His wife?"

His face lit up, and he sighed and shook his head. It was all very French. "*Mais, oui*, his taste in women is as fine as his taste in wine and food. Beautiful! *Très belle!*" I was nodding and I could feel my mouth working, but no words came out. He said, "So I can recommend some restaurants in the area."

He rattled off some names which Gallin made a note of while I frowned at the vines he had been gazing at a moment before. When he was done, he stood, and we stood with him.

"Now, if you will excuse me, I have work I must do today without fail. Anything you need, please do not hesitate to call me. You have my telephone, you just call, 'Eh, Mylan, I need this or that!' I will do my best to help."

He gave a little bow and left. As his figure disappeared from view along the gravel path, Gallin held up her glass and squinted at it.

"I think this grape has hallucinogenic qualities. I had a *really* surreal moment there."

"Me too."

"Nero is *married?*"

"Not just married, Gallin. Married to a really beautiful woman."

She nodded. "*Très belle!* Beautiful."

I shook my head. "Okay, Mrs. Beaumont, let's go change for dinner and start working on these restaurants. I am keen to meet this Mr. da Silva."

As it happened, when I was splashing on my aftershave and Gallin was pulling on a blue silk number, my phone rang. It was Mylan.

"Mr. Beaumont, I hope I do not catch you in a bad moment."

"Not at all, Mylan. How can I help you?"

He gave an embarrassed laugh. "Actually, it is my desire to help you. I have made enquiries, and I can tell you that Monsieur da Silva is dining tonight at Ponte

Sull'Arac, in Le Port. It is a wonderful restaurant in a very, very small village. So nice! The chef is superb. You will love it."

"Where is it, Mylan?"

Voila! You are taking the D six one eight south, pon, pon, pon, you are taking many curves through the forest until you are come to Massat. Here you turn left on the D eighteen, pon-pon-pon, here the road is more straight, and after three and a half kilometer you are there. You will see a small bridge on your right, over the river Arac. There is the restaurant."

We took the Range Rover, and it was pretty much as he had said. The first leg of the journey was through very dense woodland, and even though the sun had not yet set, I had to use the headlights. After Massat, the road was straighter, and the trees did not form a virtual tunnel as they had before. All the way we followed the river Arac on our right-hand side as it flowed among intense green fields and dark forests.

Le Port was tiny, maybe a dozen houses dotted over the mountainside. A small stone bridge, barely big enough for a car, spanned the foaming river. On the far side, the road became a dirt track, and immediately on the left was the restaurant.

It was a large, very basic stone house with a gabled roof and a big, bare stone chimney from which aromatic smoke trailed like it wasn't in a big hurry to get anywhere. It was the kind of place that, if the *New York Times* or the *Washington Post* ever got a hold of it, would be lost forever.

Inside, there was a log fire burning. A high ceiling was supported on sturdy wooden beams, the tables had gingham tablecloths, and each one had a different, miniature petroleum lamp. There were two tables occupied, and none of the occupants looked like they were about to unleash a virus on the world.

A waiter with a long, black apron approached us and guided us to a table by the fire.

He held Gallin's chair, and we sat at right angles to each other, so we could both see the room. I asked the waiter in broken French if M de Silva had arrived yet.

"*Mais, non, monsieur.*" He glanced over at a table that had been set up for six and had the reserved sign on it. "Are you dining with him?"

"No, I was just hoping to discuss the Manseng grape with him, but I see he has a party…"

I trailed off. He shrugged with his shoulders, his eyebrows, and his moustache. It's something only the French know how to do.

"Perhaps if monsieur would like, I can perhaps mention to him…I don't know…"

"That would be extremely kind. I would be very grateful. Meantime, we'll have a couple of martinis while we study the menu."

Forty-five minutes later and two martinis down, we were halfway through a shared cast-iron dish of mussels in cream, white wine and garlic when Humberto entered. He didn't come in. The people with him came in. He entered, and he entered making a noise. He was huge, six-three with a massive bald head, a barrel chest, and arms and legs like tree trunks. But what was really vast was his presence. He was like Orson Welles on steroids. He opened his arms wide as the head waiter hurried toward him and his guests squeezed past, and bellowed, "*Marcel! Marcel! Mon grand ami! Qu'as-tu pour mois ce soir?*"

Gallin looked at me. "What's he saying? We're all

excommunicated?"

"He is asking Marcel, the head waiter, what he has for him this evening."

I watched as Marcel groveled and Humberto and his guests swarmed to the reserved table. Humberto, seated at the head, listened carefully while Marcel explained the intricacies of what he had for him "*ce soir.*"

"I am having trouble," I said, mopping mussel juice with a hunk of baguette, "imagining that guy and Nero in this small restaurant at the same time."

"Kind of surreal. Do you think it ever happened?"

"It's a freaky thought, like the good twin and the evil twin."

For the next hour, he boomed in five languages through four courses which included six dozen oysters, freshly made salmon pâté, roasted duck with blackberry and orange purée, Argentine sirloin with *pommes de terre à la paysanne* (sliced potatoes stewed in olive oil with garlic, onion, and green peppers) and three cheese boards. They drank Krug champagne and six bottles of L'Ermita 2020, from Priorat in Catalonia, which I happened to know came in at close to two thousand bucks a bottle. With the cheese, Marcel brought out a bottle of Napoleon Brandy which he had especially for da Silva.

By that time, Gallin and I were finishing our Bushmills and Stilton. I asked Marcel for the bill, he brought it and apologized, "I did not see the right moment, monsieur, I am desolate!"

I told him not to worry, overtipped him, and on the way to the door I stepped over to da Silva's table and offered him a little bow. His eyes glanced at me but took Gallin in in detail.

"I hope you will excuse me, Mr. da Silva. I had

wanted to offer you a dessert wine from our vineyard, but seeing that superb cognac you have, it would be an impertinence."

He spoke to me, but he was still surveying Gallin. "You have a vineyard?"

Gallin answered. "We have just bought it. Well, Art bought it as a present for me. We have renamed it Chateau Beaumont. It's not far from Boussenac."

He arched an eyebrow and shifted his gaze to me. "Boussenac? There are not many vineyards in the mountains, Mr. Beaumont. The only vineyard I can think of near Boussenac belonged to another American." His eyes shifted to the ceiling in thought. "A Mr. Green. A big man with a good appetite and good taste in wine. I believe he cultivated the Manseng grape." He gestured to me with his upturned palm. "This is why you speak of the dessert wine."

I smiled. "Exactly, though we hope to develop table wines too."

"With the Manseng grape?" He pulled down the corners of his mouth and gave a small shrug. "Perhaps. Personally, I do not see it, but I will be interested to see how you get on."

"I will be delighted to let you know. But we mustn't keep you from your guests. Enjoy the rest of your—"

"Can I find you online? Facebook, the telephone directory...?"

That caught me off guard, and Gallin answered. "I don't know if we are up yet, but—" She reached in my jacket and pulled out my pen. She grabbed his napkin and wrote the chateau telephone number on it, then added, "Arthur and Anne." As she wrote, she told him, "Do call. It would be so nice to hear from you."

He held her eye, and there was no mistaking his meaning when he said, "I shall, you can be quite sure."

We stepped out into the night. There was a young moon hanging over the pine forest, touching the tops of the trees with light and making the sky translucent. Its light also reflected off two gleaming Range Rovers parked a little way up the road. Leaning against them were two men, both smoking and watching us. We ignored them, and Gallin made a show of gripping my arm and leaning her head on my shoulder as we walked to our own vehicle.

"I can't wait to try out that four-poster bed," she said, loud enough for them to hear.

We climbed in and slammed the doors.

"I'm all for playing the part of a couple madly in love with each other," I told her. "But those guys probably don't speak English."

"Oh, I wasn't playing a part," she said. "I mean it." I fired up the engine and pulled away, smiling. "Really?"

"Sure! You don't mind taking the couch tonight, do you?"

SEVEN

I t was as we were approaching Massat on the way back that I noticed the headlights in my mirror. They were too far behind us to be able to identify the car, and there was no reason right then to think it was a tail. But as we approached Massat and I slowed and turned right, I kept the speed down as we headed up into the hairpins and the closed tunnels of trees.

Behind me, I saw the headlights turn and follow and, just for a moment, in the moonlight I saw it was another Range Rover. Gallin had noticed me eyeing the rearview and turned in her seat to look. I asked her, "Do you think everybody in Occitan has a Range Rover?"

"Only the bad guys and us. Everybody else has Toyotas."

"I'm going to pull over and let him pass. Try and get a look at him."

I found a small clearing by the side of the road and pulled in beside the trees. Gallin turned in her seat to watch the bend in the road behind us. I opened my window. She whispered, "*He's coming!*" and grabbed a hold of me like we were making out. I couldn't see a damned thing, but she had a clear view out the window.

The Range Rover came around the bend, slowed

as it passed us, and moved on. She slid back into her seat and smiled. "It was one of the two guys outside the restaurant."

"He sent him to follow us. What the hell for?"

She shrugged. "To confirm we are who we say we are?"

I shook my head as I pulled away. "No, there are easier and more subtle ways to do that."

"He wants us to know he's watching us?"

I glanced at her. My face said I didn't think so, but I said, "Maybe."

We didn't see him for the rest of the drive, and there was no sign of him when we got back to the chateau. But when I parked up outside the front door, Ferrer was there to meet us. As we climbed the steps, he wasn't smiling. He gave me the thumbs up and asked, "*Okay? Todo okay?*"

I nodded. Occitan is a mixture of Spanish, French, and Catalan, so I thought I'd have a go in my schoolboy Spanish and asked him why the question, "*Si, todo okay. Por que?*"

"Man." He pointed down to the gate, then made driving motions. "*Carri.*" Then he made hand motions like stopping. "*Aplantar.*" Then he put his finger to his eye and pointed around him, "*Gaitar—*"

I pointed to our Range Rover. "*Carri?*"

He nodded." "*Si! Si!* Range Rover."

"Stop? *Aquí?*" I pointed to the gate.

"*Si*, stop *aquí.*"

"And look?" I made like a red Indian with my hand over my eyebrows, scanning the horizon. He nodded a lot. I turned to Gallin. "The son of a bitch was here, looking around." I patted him on the shoulder. "*Gracias.*"

He thumped his chest. "*Ieu aver fusilh!*" He made a motion like shooting a rifle.

I gave him the thumbs up. "Good, *bueno.*" I turned to Gallin. "He says he has a rifle, *fusil* is rifle in Spanish."

"No shit, Sherlock!"

Through a little more agonizing basic communication, he let us know he was going to be on watch all night and that there was video from the gate camera showing our friend inspecting the area.

Gallin and I took shifts. She slept four hours, and I kept watch. Then I slept, and she kept watch. All night, we both heard Ferrer patrolling the house and the grounds. In the morning, after a long, cold shower, we went down for breakfast. I told Ferrer to go get me the DVD with the footage of Humberto's man on it and then get some sleep. When he'd left, I told Gallin, "I'm going to see Humberto. I'm going to show him the security footage and ask him what the hell he thinks he's playing at."

She put some toast in her mouth and chewed, frowning at me. "You think that might lead to an invitation to join the Band of Bovine Brothers?"

"It might be a step in the right direction. Rich and aggressive might appeal to him, if I allow him to persuade me there was no harm meant."

"The Brotherhood of Bleating Baphomets."

"Drink more coffee and listen. I don't want you to come."

"I agree. I'll distract him. This has to be a macho thing. He'll like that." She watched me eat a slice of toast and drain my coffee, then asked, "How long do I wait before I call the cavalry?"

"I wouldn't expect to be there for more than half an hour, twenty minutes there, twenty back. Say two hours tops I should be back. If I'm not, call me on my cell."

Ferrer appeared with the DVD from the security camera and set it before me on the table. I asked him, "*Ferrer, Señor Green pistola?*" I made my hand like a pistol.

He nodded. "Si, si."

He gestured me to go, and I followed him to the library. Gallin came behind me. At the far end, he pulled a bunch of keys from his pocket and opened a cabinet. Inside there was a series of drawers lined in purple baize. Here, Nero, or Mr. Green as he was here in Occitan, had a collection of pistols. Mostly classic revolvers with pearl handles and fancy stuff like that, but also a Smith & Wesson 29 and a couple of Sig Sauer P226s.

I smiled at Ferrer and thanked him. Then I put my hands together beside my head and made the universal mime for sleeping. He nodded, chuckled, and left for his room in the basement. While Gallin hunkered down and started inspecting the weapons, I snooped around till I found a drawer with ammo and magazines and selected one for the Sig.

Gallin said, "Mr. Green is married to a beautiful woman and he collects classic guns. This Peacemaker is engraved with the name William Cody. We are getting a whole new inside look at the man."

I rammed the magazine in and paused to look at her. "He is a very private man," I said. "Doing this is totally out of character for him."

She met my gaze and nodded. "He believes this is for real."

I ran down the steps to the Range Rover, which was still parked out front, and five minutes later, I was driving fast along the same road I had followed the night before. I came to Massat, turned left, and moments later, I was blasting past the restaurant by the bridge. Most of the drive was through hillsides sprawling with dense forest, but after maybe half an hour, I came out of the woods above the lush, green valley of Sentenac, and up on my left, at the top of a sharp, strangely bare mountain towering over the village, was the castle. It stood, gray stone with a tall, narrow, castellated tower, dark against the blue sky. I couldn't see any windows, only the narrow slits for the archers. I followed the winding road through the village. Here too the houses were tall, made of stone, with small windows against the cold.

At the exit, I came to a huge, life-size crucifix painted blood red. Suspended from it was that poor man, nailed hand and foot. Just beyond the crucifix, there was a crossroads. The old wooden sign there said if I went right I would come to the town of Orus, but if I took the path less taken, to the left, I would come to Castèl Coudrey.

I ground up the dirt track across the face of that strangely bare mountainside until finally I came to the vast, arched wooden doors of the castle. There was a camera beside the door, and an intercom beneath it. I buzzed, and a voice like a painful throat disease said, "*Oui.*"

"This is Arthur Beaumont. I need to talk to Mr. Humberto da Silva urgently. And I mean now."

There was silence for a count of three, then, "Moment."

Five minutes passed and I was playing with the idea of shooting out the one-foot cast-iron lock on the giant doors, when the voice said, "Okay," and the giant doors buzzed and began slowly to swing open. I climbed back in the Range Rover and drove through the massive arch into a cobbled courtyard. The huge keep was directly ahead of me, and to my left was what was obviously the palatial house.

As I swung down from the cab, a big guy in an expensive suit and a ponytail stepped out to watch me. I approached him, and he held out a hand to make me stop. I knew what was coming, the question and the frisk.

"Why you want see Lord Chudleigh?"

"That's none of your goddamn business. It's a private matter between me and him. Now where is he?"

He jerked his chin at me and gestured I should raise my arms. I sighed and did so, and ten seconds later he was showing me my Sig.

"What this?"

I squinted at him. "What do you mean, what is it? It's a Sig Sauer P226 semi-automatic. Can't you read?"

He was getting mad and trying not to show it. "Why you bring weapon to see Lord Chudleigh?"

"I take it everywhere, not just to see Lord Chudleigh. Now you hang on to it if you want to till I am done. But I want to see Humberto da Silva, and I mean to see him now!"

He turned, and I followed him into the house. We crossed a very large, stone-flagged floor, went down a corridor that was wide enough to drive a truck down, and came to another arched, wooden door. He knocked, opened the door, and gestured with his head for me to go in.

Humberto was sitting at a desk the size of a small room. It was heavy, weathered ancient wood with a red hue and lots of ink stains. He was watching me with a curious frown. The guy with the ponytail moved ahead of me and laid the Sig on the desk, then stood back.

I drew breath, but he got there first. "You come to see me armed?"

"I go everywhere armed." I pulled the DVD from my pocket and dropped it on his desk. "Apparently I am wise to do so."

He lowered his gaze to take in the DVD in its plastic case. He didn't touch it. "What is this?"

"It's the driver you sent after us last night, snooping around my gate and my house. And I would like you to explain to me what in the hell *he* was doing, and what in the hell *you* were doing sending him there!"

I was surprised to see his pale, flabby cheeks color. But I knew it was not embarrassment. It was anger. There was real rage in his face as he stared at the plastic case and the DVD. After a moment, he took a deep breath and smiled. He spread his hands wide and said, "You are, of course, Mr. Beaumont, perfectly correct." He gestured to my gun. "Please, take your gun and put it away. I did send Sergio to make sure you were who you said you were, and to have a look at the chateau. A man in my position has many enemies and lives with many risks. I have learned to be very careful."

"Well, I have to tell you I am pretty damned mad. I am going to review the security in the damned place, I *will* have dogs, and you had better remember I am an American, and if I find a trespasser on my grounds at night, you can be damned sure I'll blow his goddamned head off. Do I make myself clear?"

His eyebrows were high on his forehead. "Amply, very much so. My dear fellow, you will certainly not have any trespassers from me, and I am quite sure Sergio did not actually enter your property, did he?"

I grabbed the Sig and shoved it in the holster under my arm. "I don't know, but I do know he got damned close and he was inspecting my gate. What was he doing that for? He liked the style, or he was casing the lock and the security?"

He sighed heavily, closed his eyes, and nodded.

"Mr. Beaumont, I repeat my most sincere apologies. He certainly should not have inspected your gate in that way, and those were certainly not my instructions." He gestured to the chair in front of where he was sitting. "Will you please sit, Mr. Beaumont?"

I hesitated a moment and sat, making a face that said I wasn't happy about it. He went on.

"I will reprimand Sergio in the severest terms. But will you allow me to try to make it up to you and your charming wife? Will you please accept my invitation to dine with me and some of my friends tomorrow night? You would do me a great honor. We can discuss your vineyard and we can get to know each other as neighbors and friends."

I made a big show of sighing and gave him a reluctant smile. "Well, you are every bit the gentleman, Mr.—" I hesitated a moment then said, "Can you believe I don't really know what to call you?"

I laughed, and he offered me a face of tolerant amusement. "Oh, the Lord hath many names!" He laughed again. "Some people call me my lord, others Lord Humberto, though that is quite incorrect, some Lord Chudleigh, which is correct but I don't often use that title. If you will allow me to call you Arthur, why don't you call me Humberto?"

"Well, that sounds like a very handsome offer, as

does your invitation to dinner. I know Anne will be thrilled."

I stood, and we shook, and the ponytail led me back to the Range Rover and opened the big doors for me. As I opened the driver's door to get in, he said, "Mr. Beaumont, don't bring gun again."

I smiled and looked down at the ground a second before answering. "If I do, it'll be because I plan to shoot you with it."

I got in and left.

On the way down the hill, I called Gallin. She answered immediately.

"Hello, darling."

"That man," I said, "whatever else he may be, he is a first-class gentleman. He apologized unreservedly, said he would reprimand the guy, whose name is Sergio, and has invited us to dine with him and some of his friends tomorrow night. What do you think of that?"

"Well, I think my man don't hang about?"

"What do you say I collect you and we pop down to Perpignan so you can buy yourself a dress for the occasion."

"Oh baby, you spoil me. But you won't regret it."

We exchanged a few nauseating love-you, love-you-mores, and I hung up. I knew from the conversation that she'd had the same hunch I had: Somehow we were being listened to, and Sergio's visit had been for that purpose, to plant listening devices.

EIGHT

Luz had driven out to Hagin da Silva Biotech on Bordeaux Drive, in Lakewood, as soon as he had called her to say he had to go to London that night. It hadn't taken her long. They lived less than thirty miles from Biotech, in Silver Creek. At that time of night in her 718 Boxster, she burned up 101 in less than twenty minutes, and now she was sitting on his desk pouting at him and smelling of gin.

"You leave me alone all the time these days, Sean. How long you gonna be?"

He was packing a small leather bag with a change of suit and a few essentials. He gestured to it. "I don't know exactly. A day or two. You can see what I'm packing."

"You gonna see Oscar?"

"Not if I can avoid it, Luz."

"Sean, please, he is your brother-in-law. He is havin' a real bad time over in England."

Sean took some chinos from a drawer, rolled them, and stuffed them in his bag. He couldn't remember the last time he'd dressed at home. A week, at least. "He's your brother, Luz, he's not my brother, whatever the law says. I know what he wants, and I am not going to pay for his habit, and neither are you. I told you, if he wants to go into detox, I will help him. But I am *not* paying for his filthy habit. That's an end of it."

She changed from a pout to a sad face. "You're a good man, Sean. I don't deserve you. You work so hard and all I do is give you problems."

She slid from the desk and crossed to where he was cramming a toilet bag in among his clothes. She took hold of his face and gave him a long kiss, then whispered in his ear, "We got time?"

He smiled and shook his head. "They're fueling the plane right now. As it is, by the time I get to London, it will be two or three in the morning."

"Okay, listen, Sean, please do me a favor. Mama sent me a Bible she wants me to give to Oscar. She still thinks he's here."

"Jesus! You have to tell her."

"I will, I will, but listen to me. She is ill, Papa is dead, and now she wants me to give Oscar a special Bible to remember the words of the Lord and help him find the true path. What can I tell her, 'Yes, Mama, but Oscar's gone to England'? Will you give him the Bible?"

"I told you, Luz. I won't have time!"

"You just tell me your hotel, and he will come to you. You give him the book and he is gone. For Mama."

He sighed heavily, caught sight of the clock on his wall, and said, "Fine, okay, give me the Bible and I'll give it to him. I'll be staying at the Dorchester."

She gave three little jumps, clung to him, and kissed him. "You are the best man in the whole *world!* Mama will be so happy when I tell her he has it."

She went to her handbag and extracted a gift-

DAVID ARCHER

wrapped package four inches long, three inches wide, and two inches deep. It had a ribbon and a bow, and a tag stuck to it that said, *"Para Oscar de Mama."*

She squeezed it into his bag and kissed him again. "Okay," she told him, still holding his face, "Mr. Big International Executive, I'll be waiting for you when you come back. I'll buy something nice to wear."

She turned and grabbed her bag and made for the door.

"You're not going to see me to the plane?"

She pouted. "It will only make you waste time, and it will make me cry."

She blew him a kiss and was gone. For just a moment, he could hear his own mother's voice, and see her furious Irish face: "Don't expect me to go to your feckin' wedding! If you marry a feckin' whore, you know what you'll be for the rest of you God-forsaken life? You'll be a john! A feckin' john for the rest of your miserable life!"

He pushed the thought aside and walked the short distance to the airfield. He was a frequent flier, and security knew him and waved him through. He ran across the tarmac to where he could see the Biotech plane waiting. He sprinted up the steps where the stewardess and the captain welcomed him, and within five minutes they were taxiing for takeoff. He popped a sleeping pill and settled for the flight.

Eight hours later, as they were coming in to land in the early hours of the morning, the stewardess awoke him gently with a cup of coffee. She knew his habits and his needs by now. He smiled and thanked her.

"We may have a short delay, Mr. Hagin. Apparently, there is a security alert at City Airport. They are keeping it discreet, but they are on orange alert."

He swore and stretched and watched the lights through the window as they descended through the dark.

Twenty minutes later, he was being ushered into the VIP channel through the security checks toward passport control. He entered a passage with a desk in it, and behind the desk was a man in his thirties with a uniform and a face like a bad Monday morning.

"Good morning, sir."

Sean essayed a smile. "Good morning," he answered and made to walk through. The guy in the uniform pointed to his bag. "May I see your bag, sir?"

He was genuinely surprised. It had never happened to him before. He raised it and looked at it. "This one?"

There was no expression on the guy's face when he answered. "That's the only one you've got, sir."

"Right." He gave a small laugh. "Sure, no problem."

He put it in the desk, and the guy nodded at the zipper. "Would you open it for me please, sir?"

He sighed. "Sure."

The guy was watching him. "Is there a problem, sir?"

He shook his head. "No." Again the small laugh. "I'd just love to get to my hotel. It's been a long day."

"Shouldn't take a moment."

He took out the pair of chinos, unrolled them, felt the pockets, and set them aside. He reached in, pulled out a shirt, unrolled it, and set it on the chinos. He reached in again and pulled out a suit jacket, went through the same process and reached in again. This time, he pulled out the gift-wrapped Bible.

"What is this, sir?"

"It's a present from my wife's mother to her son, my brother-in-law. He lives in London. It's a Bible."

"Would you unwrap it for me please, sir?"

"Really? Seriously?"

The guy didn't like that. Nothing changed on his face. It was expressionless anyway. But his eyes went hard.

"Yes, sir. Seriously."

He sighed again and tore the paper off. Inside there was a dark blue book. The edges of the pages were gold and written on the cover was *The Sacred Bible*. He held it up for the guy to see.

"A Bible," he said.

"Could you open it please, sir."

He rolled his eyes and groaned. "For God's sake, I am the CEO of a billion-dollar corporation. What the hell do you—"

He opened the book and froze. The center of the pages had been cut away, leaving a hollow space at the center of the book. Sitting inside that space was a plastic bag full of creamy white powder.

"What were you saying, sir? What the hell did I what?" He didn't wait for an answer. He spoke into his radio. Two minutes later, Sean was escorted to an office in the bowels of the airport and was sat at a table. A uniformed cop stood at the door, and a plainclothes officer entered and sat across the table from him. As he sat, he said, "Mr. Hagin, when the customs officer inspected your bag, he found a plastic sachet of white powder concealed in a Bible which you said was a gift for your brother-in-law. Do you agree with the statement I have just made?"

"Yes, of course I do."

"Will you tell me please what that powder is?"

"In all probability it's cocaine. I don't know for sure."

"Why don't you know, Mr. Hagin?"

"Because my wife gave it to me just before I boarded the flight. She said it was a gift of a Bible from her mother to my wife's brother. He has a cocaine habit."

"Mr. Hagin, I am not going to arrest you right now, but I am going to detain you for the next twenty-four hours while we look into this. Do you understand that?"

"Of course I understand it. I can make a phone call, right?"

The plainclothes guy nodded. "Yes, you can make a phone call."

He dialed, and it rang several times before Humberto's very sleepy voice answered.

"Sean, are you out of your mind? Do you know what time it—"

"I have been arrested."

"*What?*"

"Luz placed some cocaine in my luggage disguised as a Bible. Her brother was to come to the hotel and collect it."

"This is completely unacceptable. This is completely *impossible!*"

"I know. I'll have to... I can't think right now. You have to get me out of this."

"Where are you?"

"At City Airport in London."

"Where will they hold you?"

Sean turned to the plainclothes guy. "Where will I be held so my partner can send my attorney?"

"You'll be taken from here to Plaistow Police Station, on Barking Road. There you will be processed and held in custody for twenty-four hours. After that we will either release you or charge you."

"Did you hear that?"

"Yes, let me speak to him."

Sean held out the telephone. "He wants to talk to you."

The cop shook his head. "We'll talk to your solicitor when he—"

"He's a commissioner for the European Commission. He's a lawyer."

The detective reached for the phone and put it on speaker. "Yes, sir."

"I shall be sending a solicitor to attend to my partner's arrest. He will arrive within the next two hours. Mr. Hagin's telephone contains highly confidential and classified information which is partly the property of the United States Government and partly the property of the European Union. The telephone must not be touched by anybody but handed over to the solicitor the moment he arrives. Is that all clearly understood?"

"Yes, sir. Naturally you'll need a court order. Until then, they remain in police custody, or until Mr. Hagin is released." He handed back the phone.

Things proceeded then pretty much as the plainclothes detective had outlined. A couple of cops removed Sean to a police car. Because he was not under arrest but merely being held, out of courtesy to the European Commission and in recognition of his status as the CEO of a billion-dollar corporation, he was not cuffed. He was sat in the back of a car and driven to a large, depressing redbrick building on Barking Road, E13.

By the time he was processed and taken down to his cell, the sun had already risen, and he had sunk into a deep depression. It was so much worse than what his mother had said. He could go to prison, for years. It could bring Biotech to its knees. The damage to the company and its future relationships with China and Russia was inconceivable.

He sat on the bench looking at the walls. They were painted a grotesque yellow. Brown stains turned out to be feces, and somehow somebody had smuggled in an indelible marker and drawn obscene pictures.

At eight a.m., the big steel door opened and the guard allowed in a man in a three-piece suit. He was of average height with gray hair and had with him an attaché case. The guard said, "Any trouble, just shout, bang on the door."

The door closed, and the man sat next to Sean on the bench.

"You're my attorney, right?"

He nodded and spoke in a quiet voice. "Humberto sent me." He flipped open the case, and Sean saw his cell and his passport. "I had a court order so I have been able to recover your telephone and your other possessions. They were extremely important, as you know."

"Yeah, I know. Are you going to be able to bail me and get me off this charge?"

The man smiled. "That won't be necessary."

"You don't understand. I have *really* important work I need to do today. Did Humberto not explain that to you?"

While Sean was talking, the man in the suit had extracted an exquisite cardboard box, no bigger than an eggcup. It was tied with a bow and displayed the name of a Belgian confiseur. He smiled, opened it, and handed it to Sean.

"Humberto insisted I bring you this. It is a single Belgian chocolate. He told me to tell you that if ever you have trusted his ability to make miracles happen, then you should eat this chocolate. I was not to leave until I had seen you do so."

"Is it fr—"

He put his finger to his lips, then made the gesture for eating and waited until Sean had put the chocolate in his mouth, chewed it and swallowed it.

"It's delicious, but I'm not really in a condition to appreciate it. This is not a game. I really need to know what's happening."

"I am instructed to assure you that Humberto has everything in hand, and you are not to worry. Be confident. Everything will be resolved."

Sean wanted to answer. He wanted to tell this attorney that there was no room for complacency. He had important work to do that very day. But his limbs were heavy and did not seem to be able to respond. He watched the man collect the box and the wrapper and place them in his case. Then the man was taking hold of Sean's ankles and drawing his feet up onto the bench. His body slid back. A desperate panic welled up inside him as it dawned on him that he was completely paralyzed.

The face came very close to his, and he saw for the first time the unutterable evil in those pale blue eyes.

"Best thing you can do now, Mr. Hagin, is embrace the inevitable and go to sleep."   The man brushed his hand over Sean's eyelids and closed them. A moment later, he banged on the door, and it was opened by the same guard. Sean heard the man's voice, "The poor fellow is exhausted. He asked to sleep. I told him I'd be back in a couple of hours."

He heard the door slam and the voices depart, while he screamed in his mind, while death closed in and slowly the muscles that allowed him to breathe ceased to work.

Meanwhile, nine thousand miles away, Luz Hagin awoke from a drunken sleep to see, by the fading light of the moon filtering through the open terrace doors, a small man with a pointed face, gray hair, and very thin legs leaning over her. She trembled violently and drew breath to scream.

The blade he used was an especially adapted scalpel. He drove it through her throat, right through her neck, so that it severed the vertebrae at the back and cut the spinal nerve. He kept smiling at her. He knew that the brain would continue living and thinking for a short while after the body had ceased to function.

As he saw the life fade from her eyes, he said, "Goodbye."

NINE

There was a fire burning in a fireplace that was big enough to have a party in. It was made of hewn gray stone, and the logs were the size of small trees. Humberto da Silva was all about being big.

The table at which we sat was not long, but it was big. Gallin was on his right-hand side, and he held her hand at every chance. On his left was the Marchioness of Quillan. I sat beside her, and opposite me was Paul Van Brook, who owned diamond mines in South Africa. Opposite Humberto, and on my left, was a pretty Hollywood actress turned producer called Sandy, who was a billionaire three times over.

We had had cocktails in one of the drawing rooms, watching the sunset over the mountains, and then we had proceeded into the magnificent dining room. There we had been treated to rainbow trout simmered in butter with rosemary and dried figs, accompanied by his ubiquitous Krug champagne, and now we had an entire Argentine sirloin on the credenza beside the table, and two very skilled men with white mushroom hats were slicing filets and brazing them over scalding coals right there beside the fire. As they were distributed, Humberto would shout, laughing, "Do not wait! Do not wait! Eat them while they are hot and juicy!"

And while he shouted, pretty young maids distributed carrots Vichy and boiled new potatoes in garlic, butter, and parsley. The wine was a seemingly endless supply of *Carruades de Lafite* from 2016.

"Did you hear, Paul?" Humberto said suddenly. "My partner in Biotech was murdered."

Paul had a hunk of nearly raw meat halfway to his mouth, but he stopped, gaping, and laid his fork down.

"Sean, Sean Hagin? He was *murdered?* Is the world going *crazy?* I mean, that's—" He glanced at me and stopped. "I mean that's awful. I am so sorry."

"Murdered, indeed, but my dear chap. The worst of it is that he was murdered *in a police cell!*"

His expression as he took in the table and all the gasps was triumphant. I glanced at Gallin, and she told me with her eyes she'd gotten it too. It was the Marchioness of Quillan who asked the question everybody else wanted to ask.

"What in the name of God was he doing in a police cell in the first place? I met him, and he was perfectly charming."

"You will forgive me, Marchioness, but I am beholden to the truth. He was the victim of the treachery of women!"

Sandy, sitting next to me, laughed just a little and said, "What can you mean, Humberto?"

"He was on his way to London. You know we own Biotech together, though he was the CEO. Anyway, he had some business of his own over there, and when he gets off the plane, some officious border guard makes him open his hand luggage. Turns out his wife has slipped in a Bible."

The Marchioness of Quillan echoed, "A *Bible?* That *whore?*"

We all laughed. Humberto, laughing, said, "But it was no ordinary Bible, my dear marchioness. This Bible contained two hundred grams of pure cocaine! Pure *gasolina!*" He leaned back in his throne-like chair and threw his hands in the air. "Now, explain to those British border guards, 'No, you see, Officer, it was put there by my wife for her brother! It has nothing to do with me!'"

The Marchioness of Quillan was shaking her head so hard she made her tiara rattle. "As soon as I met them. He was charming, civilized, almost European. But she! *Mon dieu!* The filth of Colombia!"

"That doesn't explain," said Sandy, "how he got himself iced in the cooler, if you'll excuse my inappropriate humor."

"Humor is never better than when it is inappropriate, my darling Sandy. It is something of a mystery. He was not arrested and charged. They were holding him while they made further inquiries. His British solicitor apparently went to see him, and they talked. The solicitor left and everything was apparently fine, except that Sean had told him he was tired and wished to sleep. But when the guards next checked on him, he was dead, poisoned with curare."

I was getting bored, so I decided to join the conversation and see if I could ruffle a few feathers. I spoke up just as Paul was opening his mouth. "Looks like somebody somewhere has got himself a stash of curare." They all looked at me. I shrugged and spread my hands, still holding my knife and fork. "Curare is rare and not that easy to get hold of. When was the last time you heard of somebody getting poisoned with curare, unless it was in a book or a movie?" I sawed off a piece of steak and put it in my mouth. "Now we have two in less than a week."

I picked up my glass, staring straight at Sandy. "You must have heard about it. In Los Angeles, Frazer Benson was drugged with curare before he was ritually tortured and executed. And now, less than a week later, your partner, Sean Hagin."

Sandy looked at me with interest. "You're very well informed, Arthur. Is this a hobby of yours?"

"Poisoning?" I laughed out loud. "No, poisoning is a woman's way of killing, so I'm told. Am I right, honey?" I asked Gallin across the table.

She giggled. "I never killed anyone with poison."

"I love the ambiguity," I told her. "No, anyone I have ever killed," I said, "has been with a firearm, a blade, or my bare hands."

There were lots of raised eyebrows. Paul burst out laughing. "My God! How many men have you killed?"

I shrugged. "I lost count. And then, in combat you don't always see the people you're shooting with automatic fire. I guess after a time, you get habituated."

Paul was nodding sagely. "I have never killed a man. But I have killed big game, lions, elephants, and I tell you the first few times, it really has an impact on you, but over time..." He trailed off because I was shaking my head. "You don't agree?"

"There is no comparison, Paul. Killing an animal, even a large mammal, you're aware it's a different species, there is no real *connection*. But you hold a human being up close and look into their eyes as you drive a knife into their throat or their heart, or you break their neck with your hands, you *connect* with that person. That is a real confrontation with reality."

Humberto said, "And you were able to do it again."

I held his eye and said, "And again. Sometimes you have to"—I shrugged—"to save your life, to save somebody else's life, or to defend a belief or a moral value."

They were all very quiet. After a moment, Humberto asked, "And what are your moral values, Arthur, the ones you are prepared to kill for?"

"Well." I looked at Gallin and gave her a small, private smile. "For one thing, I don't think you should ever be prepared to kill for something you wouldn't die for. Beyond that, I would say that over the years, my moral values have changed. It seems at times that all those ideals we fought for at the beginning of last century were an illusion. Every day we seem to drift further into dystopia. Freedom, justice, the rule of law, democracy..." I shook my head. "They seem to be as nothing today." I laughed. "I'm sorry, I have brought the tone down. It must be this superb wine."

"Far from it." It was Sandy, talking to me but looking at Humberto. "I think you have elevated the tone considerably, don't you, Lord Chudleigh?"

"I have to say I agree with Sandy, and I agree with you, Arthur. The values we held so dear, cultivated and fought for from the Renaissance, to the great climax of Hitler's Third Reich and the Soviet Union, have proved to be chimeras. Let us name them: freedom, democracy, the rule of law, liberty from oppression and the right to own property, the right to seek happiness, the right to life. They are chimeras not because they lack value in themselves, but because only the smallest minority of human beings want them. It is pathetic and tragic, but true."

He gestured at me and roared, "You and I, Arthur! Our souls *burn* when we think of these ideals. Our hearts and our blood are on fire! But if I had a little flying saucer now and we flew, unseen, over Paris, London, New York, or Washington, what would we see? I will tell you what we would see!" He slammed his palm down on the table and made the plates and the cutlery jump. "We would see human insects in hives, tuned in to the Hive Mind through their cell phones and their computers and their televisions, with not a single passion in their hearts except the passion for instant gratification."

He sank back in his chair with his huge hands resting on either side of his plate and observed me. When he spoke again, it was more quietly.

"You sound like a man who is disillusioned with humanity, Arthur."

I made a show of thinking about it, like the answer might be in the wine, and finally I said, "I don't think that is very far off the mark."

He grunted and made a temple of his fingers. I watched the light from the fire move in his glass and wash his big, bald head with orange light.

"I don't know," he said quietly, "if the human soul is dying in the age of silicon, or if humans have always been this way, and it is the few, the remarkable, crazy few, who have dragged this slovenly, mindless breed from age to age. A few visionaries leading the sheep toward the light."

"Both options seem as ghastly as each other. I want to believe in humanity, but I don't want to believe the human soul is dying."

He smiled, then threw back his head and laughed out loud. When he'd finished, he arched a brow at me.

"Just because only a small minority of oysters produce pearls, it does not mean you have to stop believing in oysters, Arthur."

I picked up my glass and studied the wine for a moment. "That is quite a shattering thought, Humberto."

He ignored my comment and wet on. "We must merely understand the oysters in a different way. Humanity, as a collective, has the potential to produce unique, wonderful individuals: Aristotle, Shakespeare, Mozart, Einstein. But equally it is a mistake to look at *all* humanity as a collection of unique, wonderful individuals, because they are not. They are merely the must out of which the wine will be fermented and the spirit distilled."

I stared at him. There was a horrible logic to what he was saying, and for a moment, I didn't know how to respond. Sandy sat forward and spared me the need.

"There is a lot of truth in what Humberto is saying." She turned to Paul, as though she was addressing him, but I knew the message was for me. "Pick a unique individual, Hitler, Churchill, Mozart, Picasso, Shakespeare goes without saying, and ask them a question—any question: Trump or Biden? What do you want for dinner? What's your favorite color...?"

Humberto began to laugh, nodding. She smiled at him and went on.

"The first thing he is going to do is refer *inside* for the answer. He will turn to *himself* for guidance." Paul was nodding. She turned to me. "But go to the local gas station, supermarket, DIY store, pick a person at random off the street, and ask them the same question, and the first thing they are going to do, without even being conscious of it, is refer to social media for the answer.

Failing that, they will seek some other figure to follow: Jesus, Mohammed, Buddha, Marx. It doesn't matter. They will not look to themselves for the answer."

"But why?" It was the Marchioness of Quillan. "Why are they like that? I was a communist, you know, in my youth. I *believed* in the people. But look what happened in the Soviet Union, in China and Cuba. Look what is happening now in the European Union. They are just *sheep!*"

Sandy exchanged a long look with Humberto, then cleared her throat and addressed me. "You can separate human beings into two types: those who have an 'I' and those who don't. What I mean by that is, there are those who know they are different from other people, and then there are the vast majority who feel they are part of the mass. You can tell them because when they meet at work in the morning, they will discuss what they saw on TV the night before."

Gallin spoke suddenly for the first time. "But what does this mean? I get what you're talking about, and I know Arthur does because we have talked about this many times. But where does it leave you? In the end, we may be smarter than them, but we are at their mercy. Especially in the digital age of social media. They control everything with this shared, collective hive consciousness."

Humberto leaned back, clapping and laughing. His face was a picture of joy.

"I knew I liked her from the moment I saw her. Arthur, I am going to make you an offer. With your permission, I would like to set you a test. If you pass the test, I will reveal to you and to Anne a great truth. Then I will set you a quest, and if you are successful, I will make you one of the richest men on the planet. I will set you in the pantheon of the gods. Think about it—"

"No."

He stared at me. They all did. I shook my head. I was feeling a little lightheaded, and I wanted to laugh. I attributed it to the wine and said, "I don't need to think about it. An offer like that comes once in a thousand lifetimes, if at all. It might be bullshit, in which case I have lost nothing. But what if it's true? So my answer is yes."

Humberto and Sandy gave each other a lingering smile while the marchioness looked eagerly at everyone and I forced myself not to look at Gallin. The desire to laugh was getting stronger. Eventually Humberto said, "This promises to be a most interesting evening."

He reached in his pocket and pulled out his cell. He scrolled, touched the screen, and put it to his ear. After a moment, he said, "*Portarme Sergio.*"

I frowned at him. A pellet of urgent heat burned in my belly. Humberto smiled at Gallin, and a moment later the door opened with a loud, wooden clatter and four big guys in suits pushed into the room, holding between them the man who had driven past us a couple of nights earlier and inspected our gate. He looked mad, but most of all, he looked scared. Humberto looked at me and said, "Come, Arthur. Stand."

I got to my feet and followed him to stand in front of Sergio. Humberto faced me.

"This man is a mercenary. He has raped and murdered in the service of repellent regimes all over the Third World. That is why I recruited him. He is usually efficient, very obedient, and he has no moral scruples. This is the man I sent to follow you, and it seems while he was there he contemplated the possibility of breaching your gate. None of that worries me, though I understand it may worry you." He took a step to his right and left me facing the man. "No," he went on, "what vexes me is that he failed me, and, through his carelessness, he exposed me and got caught. Therefore, I will ask you a favor. I will ask you to kill him."

TEN

Somehow I'd had a hunch what was coming when Sergio was shoved through the door, and by the time I stood up, I'd already been through my moral crisis. I detested killing a person in cold blood, but at stake here was not just finding and neutralizing the virus, but the obvious fact that if I said no, Gallin and I could not be allowed to live. I didn't hesitate.

I didn't recognize it at the time, but there was a wild craziness in me. I stepped behind him and shouldered the guards out of the way. I had brought my steak knife with me and I gripped Sergio's forehead hard with my left hand against my shoulder, drove the knife deep into the side of his neck and punched forward. I made sure the blood sprayed all over Humberto's face and his Savile Row evening suit.

He stepped back three paces, covering his face with his hands. I let the body drop to the floor and stood watching Humberto trying to wipe the blood from his face.

"Did you look in his eyes?" I asked him. He stared at me, startled, and started a shrill, almost hysterical laugh.

I returned to the table and dropped the knife beside my plate. I looked over at Gallin. Her face told me she understood. I sat. Behind me, I could hear them dragging the corpse away and issuing instructions about a mop and a bucket of water. Humberto appeared at the head of the table, still laughing.

"You will have to forgive me a moment while I change. Sandy, will you take our guests into the Sumer drawing room and arrange drinks for them? I will join you in no time."

The Sumer drawing room was next door, and called so because it was richly decorated with Sumerian artifacts, most of which looked as though they might be real. The Marchioness of Quillan sat in a large armchair by the fire. Paul sat opposite her and started a conversation about death, reincarnation, and paranormal psychic research in London. Gallin and I started a tour of the artifacts in the room, seeking a chance to be alone. I needed to tell her I felt very strange, that I felt I had been drugged. But Sandy drifted after us.

There were a few statues, not many, but there were a lot of clay tablets with inscriptions in them and larger pieces that looked like bits of wall with carved images of men with huge wings, beards, wristwatches, and handbags. Sandy's voice came soft and made Gallin turn as I opened my mouth to speak.

"It's a very dark time in the human story. It's impossible to tell myth from history. And then we find that the Bible stories originate in the Sumerian tablets."

Gallin put her hand on my arm and spoke to Sandy. "They do?"

Sandy nodded and smiled. "Are you Jewish? Abraham is the first of the Hebrew patriarchs. According to the book of Genesis, Abraham was born in Ur, in Mesopotamia, which was essentially what was left of

Sumeria. God called him to found a new nation in an undesignated land which he later learned was Canaan. Today Israel, the West Bank and Gaza, also Jordan, parts of Syria and Lebanon. He obeyed and received a covenant that his seed, supposedly the Jewish people, would inherit that land.

"What *we* believe is that Abraham brought with him the ancient history of Sumeria. What we know as Genesis and the Old Testament is a rewriting of Sumerian stories of the creation of mankind and its near extinction in the Great Flood. The true origin of humanity." She paused, holding Gallin's eye. "Who we are. We are the children of Elohim."

The desire to laugh I had had before was growing stronger. I couldn't believe the conversations I was hearing. I had just killed a man, and they were chatting about reincarnation and Sumerian gods. I wondered vaguely if I had been given acid and I was tripping. I heard Gallin say,

"The children of God?"

Sandy gave a small, pretty laugh. "No, Anne. The children of Elohim. Humberto will explain. Whiskey, cognac, or something else?"

"Bushmills," I said. Gallin glanced at me, then back at Sandy and nodded. "Yeah, Irish."

Sandy walked away and arranged drinks for us and for the marchioness and the diamond billionaire. And shortly after that, the door opened and Humberto walked in with a big grin all over his face. He glanced over at Sandy, boomed, "Armagnac, my love!" and strode over toward me with his arms outstretched.

"What a remarkable... What a remarkable..." He said it three times, then shook his head and embraced me and pounded my back with his hands.

I gave him a couple of pats and disengaged. "I was going to apologize. I feel very strange…"

"What for?" He held me by the shoulders and furrowed his brow. "Apologize for what?"

I smiled at Gallin, gave her a *what the hell?* Shrug, and gestured at his new evening suit. She burst out laughing the way only something really surreal can make you laugh. I told him, "You had to change your clothes because I made a guy spray his blood all over you." Then I added, "Humberto, it wasn't an accident. I did that on purpose."

"I know!" he said with the kind of intensity most of us reserve for winning the lottery or getting promoted to CEO. Suddenly we were all three laughing, and he was saying, "Tell me! Tell me something! What made you do it?"

I looked at Gallin again and took a deep breath. When I spoke, I was surprised to find that for the second time that evening, I was speaking the truth.

"Frankly, I hear a lot of people talk a lot of bullshit about life and death. I thought that was what you were doing. I thought I'd teach you a lesson. I'm beginning to think maybe I was wrong."

"Right, wrong, what's the difference? The important fact is, my friend, that you reached inside yourself for an answer, and acted aggressively on your environment!"

"What Humberto means," put in Sandy in her sweet voice, "is that you took the initiative and acted drawing on your own experience. You were fearless because you believed in yourself and what you were doing. You didn't turn to anyone, even your beautiful wife, for guidance or approval."

"And that," said Humberto, patting me on the shoulder, "and the extreme to which you went without hesitation, makes you a very special man indeed." He turned toward the fire and boomed at Paul and the Marchioness of Quillan.

"Go, my darlings! Your Lord must speak with his newfound brother! Go to the Rose drawing room, or go to bed, but leave us."

Paul stood and helped the marchioness to her feet, and they left the room as though we were not there. I turned to Gallin. "Are we getting in over our heads? This is deep. This is very deep." Before she could answer, I turned to Sandy. "Are we getting in too deep?"

Gallin said, "I like it, Arthur. I want to see where this leads." She came and clung to my arm and pressed herself against me. "And I have a feeling. I feel this is good for you. You need it."

Humberto sat in the big armchair to the right of the fire. Sandy came and led Gallin to the sofa, and I sat in the big chair on the left of the fire, so that Sandy and Gallin were between us. Humberto placed his hands on his knees and spoke.

"You will agree with me, Arthur, that few people today, even the most torpid and bovine, are not aware on some level that we are approaching a major crisis, perhaps even an end to civilization. The planet is hurtling toward its limit of nine billion people; we have just topped eight billion. Over half a billion people are added to the population every year. We will reach nine billion in less than two years. And the number added increases exponentially.

"We exist in a world economy, which is a

consumer economy. Do you know what this means?" He raised a hand. "The question is rhetorical. It means two fundamental things: one, that the people exist to consume, and two, that the entire economy of the world is interdependent. If it fails in one place, it fails everywhere. That would not be such a great problem if the economy were stable. But our economy is built on a credit vacuum, and within it, economies like ours, the Russian, and the Chinese are at war with each other. We are suspended, paralyzed, in a world hurtling toward human extinction."

I sipped my Bushmills and said, "That's a pretty bleak view. And for me to say that, that's something."

He raised a hand. "Please, do not interrupt me. This is not a subjective view, Arthur. This is fact. We have a choice. A choice of which we have been aware since the beginning of the Industrial Revolution, since Smith and Bentham, but we have willfully ignored. We are vastly overpopulated by the dross of humanity, which is turning our planet into hell, when it could be a paradise for the best of our kind." He paused and closed his eyes. "Can you imagine, our world, unpolluted by ugliness and ignorance, with a population of no more than two or three million people in just four or five cities? Sustained by nuclear energy, with every person educated to the highest level of sophistication, it would be a paradise."

I glanced at Sandy. She had her right arm around Gallin and placed her left index finger to her lips.

Humberto opened his eyes and skewered me with them.

"What I admired in you, Arthur, was your ruthless absence of hesitation. You saw, you understood, you felt and you acted, all in a millisecond. And that is what is called for today. For my intention is to bring this civilization to an end."

I suppressed the laugh, but I raised an eyebrow at him. He'd asked me not to speak, so I kept my mouth shut, but my face said everything there was to say.

"You think I'm insane?"

I raised my shoulders and spread my hands. It was a gesture of reluctance.

"You are a man with a lot of power and wealth, you have achieved more than most men dare to dream about, you are clearly highly intelligent. So I am trying to reserve my judgment, but you have to admit. Everything you have done and said sounds like you're out of your mind." I turned to Sandy. "Forgive me if that's offensive, but I was asked to kill a man tonight."

She didn't answer me. She still had a slight smile on her face which she turned on Humberto. He said, "And you killed him. Does that make you out of your mind too?"

I pointed to Gallin. "We are in a remote castle in the middle of the Pyrenees. You are surrounded by armed men whom you send to spy on people. You're in a position, politically and financially to bury a murder where no one will ever find it. What would you have done if I had refused to kill him? I didn't—and don't—know. With my wife here, it wasn't a risk I was prepared to take."

"And now you are willing to take that risk?"

I shook my head. "You told me you would give me a quest and make me very rich. Occasionally a very crazy, very powerful person comes along in the world, an Alexander, Julius Caesar, Ganger Rolf, Napoleon, Hitler. These people are crazy insofar as they do not accept the limitations that define other people's lives, but they make things happen. What you are describing is no crazier than the Third Reich or the Soviet revolution. So yes, I think you're out of your mind. But I also think you are rich enough, powerful enough, and brilliant enough to pull it off."

He waited, with his eyebrows slightly raised, like I had missed something. I hesitated, then nodded.

"And yeah, I think your analysis of the modern world, and the problem of overpopulation is right on the money. It's a blind alley, and we are too far down it to pull out." I took a pull on my whiskey and pointed at him as I swallowed. "So your intention is to bring this civilization to an end, presumably so that you can institute the new civilization you dream of. With that established, I have to assume that my quest has something to do with facilitating that end."

He gestured at Sandy. "My darling, why don't you?"

She turned to me. She still had her arm around Gallin's shoulders.

"Over the last decade, Humberto and I have been accumulating companies and corporations, large and small. Our defining criteria have been that the companies must operate in the fields of biotechnology, nanotechnology, information technology, and/or artificial intelligence. We have geared the research in those companies to our purpose, and where necessary, we have merged companies so that they could merge their research and development. Very recently, we have had a breakthrough."

"What kind of breakthrough?"

She ignored the question. "We were ready to deploy. But Sean Hagin's death caused us a setback. Now we are in need of a man who can step into his shoes. That is the quest. Are you ready to do it?"

I closed my eyes. My mind was racing. I said, "What kind of breakthrough? Deploy what? And how, when dealing with an operation of this magnitude, how are you prepared to put your trust in a man you barely know?"

She sat back and crossed one long leg over the other under her cream silk dress.

"Humberto?"

He raised his big, fat index finger. "A breakthrough in biological computing. We are talking about a single, living cell with the computing capacity of a million computers, able to perform the most complex operations at the speed of light. Do you know what that means? Operations at the speed of light in a space too small to be seen by the naked eye? That is what kind of breakthrough."

He sipped his Armagnac. "Deploy what? Deploy *that*. Try to imagine what it would mean for humanity if such a cell were to be weaponized into a virus. We are talking about an intelligent virus capable of conducting billions of equations per second, whose capacity for analysis, whose capacity for overcoming problems is to all intents and purposes unlimited. This is what you will deploy."

A wave of nausea washed over me. A voice in my head kept telling me this was madness, that he was insane, that such a thing was not possible. But the sick pit in my stomach kept telling me that technology had come this far and further, and the only thing holding it back was ever more frail legislation. With the rise of IT billionaires in a world which, as Humberto had said, had an ever more interdependent economy, this kind of research was not only possible, but ever more likely. And

Humberto da Silva was just the man to make it happen.

"What about my last question?"

His eyes became hooded and sly, and his smile was uncloaked evil. "Oh, Arthur, I could be very unoriginal and abduct your darling Anne. I am sure we would have lots of fun together while you were on your quest. And I can see by the way you look at her that you are quite besotted and would do almost anything for her. But wipe out over nine tenths of the human race? I think you might just draw the line at that." He shook his head. "No, I am a genius, Arthur. I have an IQ of one hundred and seventy-three, and I am particularly skilled at reading people. You are going to deploy this weapon because you want to. Because you are going to realize what it means for you, your wife, and your children. I *know* you, Arthur Beaumont. I understand, from the short time I have known you and the tests I have subjected you to, exactly how your mind works. You will do it, because you want what's best for your wife and your children."

He said it again, but I only half caught it. I looked over at Gallin. She was asleep, with her head resting on Sandy's shoulder. The fire was very warm, and I was perspiring. Somewhere I knew I had been drugged. I knew that was bad, but what surprised me and amused me was that I didn't really care much anymore. I wanted to go home. I wanted to get Gallin and take her home, but when I tried to move, my limbs were too heavy.

Then, quite suddenly, we were out among the mountains, gazing up through the pine trees at the translucent night sky and the moon. I looked down at Gallin, and she was smiling at me, and I felt a joy I had never felt before.

ELEVEN

The sun was shining. The curtains, which were lace, were rising gently, moving on the morning breeze. There was birdsong. The birds were busy and chattering out over the lawns, among the trees.

I didn't know how long I had been lying there, looking at that bright, fresh, early-morning window. It might have been hours, it might have been seconds. I didn't care. I felt good. Not caring was fantastic, in a quiet, peaceful way. I was smiling. Gradually I became aware of the presence in the bed beside me. Gallin stirred and stretched. I turned and smiled at her, became aware she had no clothes on and realized I also was undressed. Then, an image at a time, the night before began to come back to me. Or at least, parts of it did.

"What the…?"

I heard my own voice as though somebody else had spoken. I sat up. Gallin was grinning up at me as she took another stretch.

"Hey, Mr. Beaumont, when did you creep into bed?"

I half laughed. "Did we…?"

She thought about it, gazing at the window. "I dunno. I think I'd remember. It doesn't *feel* like we did. But I honestly don't remember… Man, we must have been really wrecked. Did we drink that much?"

I rubbed my face. "I don't remember. I remember patches."

She frowned. "Holy... shit! You killed that guy!" Suddenly her face lit up. It was wrong but somehow it was okay too. "You were wild. It's coming back to me. You were the *boss!*"

I swung my legs out of bed and stood. She covered her face with her fingers separated. "You going to get dressed, big guy?"

"Stand up."

She pulled the duvet about her and stood. "Now what?"

"How do you *feel*?"

She shrugged. "I feel great. Actually, I feel fantastic. How about you?"

I nodded. "Yeah, me too. Do you remember getting home?"

She thought. "Nope."

"Do you remember leaving the party?"

"Uh-uh." She shook her head. "Just kind of patchy snatches. But I *do* remember you were amazing."

I was fighting hard to sound serious, and to feel serious. I barked, "Hey!"

She giggled. "Yeah, you need to put some clothes on."

"*Hey!*"

"*What?*"

"How much do you need to drink to black out?"

She giggled. "*Lots!*"

"Right. Do you feel hungover?"

She paused. "Oh, no. I feel—"

"Great."

"Son of a bitch!" She laughed.

I went to the bathroom and stepped into the shower. As I started soaping myself, she peered in the cubicle, grinning.

"You know how I feel?"

"Get a grip. This is serious." I flicked water in her face, and we both laughed. "I mean it," I added.

"I know. But I feel—I feel *disinhibited*. Like I don't really give a damn. Shall I get in the shower with you?"

I laughed. "No!"

"Come on! You know you want me to."

She stepped in, and the water was drenching us both. I grabbed her by the shoulders and spoke fiercely, fighting the wild drive I had inside me. "You know I want this! You know there's nothing I want more in this world! But baby, if this ever happens, it will be because *we* want it. Not because some son of a bitch has drugged us and played with our minds!"

She was nodding, gripping my arms and nodding. "God, you're so intense!"

I turned away from her and turned the water to cold. It made her squeal, and I roared. After the initial shock, it felt good. I looked into her face. Her nails dug into my shoulder as she clawed me and cursed savagely, "Son of a *bitch!*"

She stormed out of the shower, and while I finished, she stood at the sink splashing cold water over her face.

We dried off and dressed in silence on opposite sides of the room.

At breakfast on the terrace, as she sipped her

coffee, she asked me, "Where did you get such self-discipline and control?"

"Upper-class white Anglo-Saxon Protestant family. We inherited that English stiff upper lip."

"I'll probably be thankful for it in a week."

"I hope I am, but somehow, I doubt it."

"Let's change the subject. How much do you remember?"

"I remember killing Sergio. He must have administered the drug by then. I justified it and explained it to myself as much as to Humberto that I was doing it to protect us and particularly you. But the fact is I was totally without inhibition. I didn't feel a thing. That's not me."

She nodded. "I felt admiration. I thought you were both cool and hot at the same time."

"Don't start."

"Okay!"

"Then I remember a lot of philosophical crap about the Bible and Sumer."

"I remember all of that. I thought it was pretty interesting."

"The upshot was that we were superior to other people because we knew who we were, and we're not part of the hive."

She took a deep breath and sighed. "You know, if I could feel anything other than…"—she waved her hand between her and me—"you know… I would feel revulsion at such an immoral idea. But actually, you know, they *are* sheep. I have often thought so. There were aspects of what they said that I could relate to."

"That's the drug talking."

"I guess—"

"I also remember him giving me a mission."

"A quest."

"A quest. I don't remember any of the details. I just remember that I had to take an intelligent virus, a biochip programmed with nano-technology, to some place. And it will wipe out more than nine-tenths of humanity."

She shook her head. "You know what? I don't believe it. It's science fiction. They are playing with our minds for some reason. It's fantasy."

"Yeah, but you know what the problem is? Our bog standard technology today makes science fiction look primitive. Science fiction today borders on fantasy, because the technology of the next ten or twenty years will be like magic. The biochips he was talking about were theoretical in the 1980s. The technology has been held back by Western legislation, but a man like Humberto is rich enough and powerful enough to invest in research in unregulated jurisdictions."

I drained my cup and refilled it.

"He owns a company that owns part of a Hong Kong company that is jointly owned by a Chinese company that owns a company in Iran, and that's where the research and development is carried out."

She laughed. "Baby, you may well be right, but I'll tell you this, we are not going to be sitting here in two weeks with nearly eight billion dead people scattered around the globe!" She picked up a croissant and went to tear it in half but threw it back in the basket and pointed at me. "And I'll tell you something else. *He* doesn't want that."

"How do you figure that?"

"The logistics! How the hell do you clean up seven thousand eight hundred million dead people? And how the hell do they protect themselves from this virus? What, it only attacks people with an IQ below one hundred and forty-five?"

"Hell, I don't know."

"They are playing with our minds. I'm telling you."

"So what should we do?"

She shrugged and picked up her broken croissant again. She thought for a moment, then laughed. "Look at it this way. One, we need to find out what he is *really* doing, assuming it is not a virus to wipe out over nine-tenths of humanity. So we go along with it. You told him you'd go on the quest. Do it."

"Go and plant the virus."

"Right. Now, worst-case scenario, everything he said is true—"

"Jesus!"

"Stay with me. Everything he said is true. So with you or without you, they are going to make it happen. They are going to wipe out seven thousand so many hundred million people, and leave just a couple of hundred million alive—if that. Right?"

I nodded. "Right."

She leaned her elbows on the table. In her right hand, she had a spoonful of blueberry jelly, and she gave me a slow once-over touched by a smile. "Well, Mr. Beaumont, if it's just a crazy mind game, we are laughing. But if it all turns out to be true, we want to be among those couple of hundred million survivors, don't we?"

I stared at her for a long time. I struggled, fought to feel something other than the desire to take her upstairs.

I knew she would come with me. I knew she wanted it as much as I did. We were on a razor's edge. I said , "Yeah, we want to be among that couple of hundred million."

She put a piece of croissant in her mouth and chewed, watching me.

"But I'm telling you this is a game these crazies are playing. Hell, maybe they're testing a new recreational drug. Crazier things happened in Stanford in the seventies. Or maybe it's an induction process into their club, like Cruise and the Scientologists, or some crap. And if that's all it is, fine, so be it. But if it's real. Think about it, baby. He said he would make you one of the richest men in the world, a prince! We gotta back the right horse here." She grinned and winked. "And I'll tell you something, big guy, if that is you without your inhibitions, you were wild last night! You are one hundred and ten percent man. I just wish I could remember the bits I don't remember!"

"Stop." I drank coffee. "Okay, so I'll call him and ask to meet and talk. See what this quest is about, preferably without half a ton of dopamine stimulants in my bloodstream."

"Go get 'em, tiger."

I picked up my cell and frowned. "Did we get his number last night?"

As I asked the question, my cell rang and the screen said, "Humberto da Silva." I held Gallin's eye for a beat and put it on speaker as I answered.

"It must be telepathy," I said. "I had just picked up the phone to call you."

His voice came back amused and slightly booming. "I am quite sure we could develop telepathy with the nano-biotech we have, but I'm afraid this is much more pedestrian than that. One of the things dear Sergio did at your house was to plant a number of very sophisticated listening devices."

I scanned the crazy conversations we had had since I'd woken up. Gallin was watching me and gave her head a microscopic shake. We'd both had that hunch, and we'd both phrased everything with care.

"So he did break in."

"Of course he did, Arthur. And in answer to your beautiful wife's analysis, I will tell you both that I do not play around. Mind games are as far beneath me as home brewing elderberry wine is beneath you. The logistics are more than taken care of."

I sighed audibly. "Okay, but we need to talk. I need to try at least to dissuade you—"

"You really don't want to bore me, Arthur. That would be an *extremely* bad idea. I don't bore well. I had hoped your experience of freezine—that is our affectionate term for it—might have opened your mind a little, but it seems your wife has made better use of it than you have."

"Yeah, well you know what Freud said, women have no superego and therefore no moral values."

"I admire your strength, Arthur. But don't miss the boat by clinging to your petty morality. Do you want to be in the five million, or do you want to be slaughtered with the sheep?"

"Five million..."

I looked up at the huge, palatial chateau, out at the perfect lawns and the dense forest. I listened to the birds singing their morning songs under the great blue dome.

Eight thousand million dead.

I said, "I want to be part..." I trailed off and shook my head. "I want to *find* my*self*, be my*self*, in a new world of free, unique individuals."

Those were the buzzwords he wanted to hear. His tone changed. It was serious, calm, even rational. "Welcome," he said. "Welcome to the Brotherhood of the Goat."

"But I need to see you, without the drugs and the alcohol. We need to talk about how we do this. What are the steps? How does it play out? And Anne had a point, what does this damn thing do, only attack people with an IQ below one forty-five?"

"Of course."

"And I need guarantees that Anne and I will be among those five million."

"Of course. You are precisely the kind of people we want. But I will give you those guarantees. Come and see me now." He chuckled. "But I should tell you, Arthur. We all take a dose of freezine every morning. It has no negative side effects, and it really gives you a wonderful perspective on life. Think about it. If it is a disinhibitor, you are *more* you when you take it, not less. It is such a shame you resisted it this morning."

I caught Gallin's eye, and she started to laugh. I closed my eyes and shook my head.

"I'll be there within the hour," I told him.

TWELVE

He had installed an elevator which took me to the office he had at the very top of the tall tower, with panoramic views of the mountains and the forests in all directions, that made you feel almost like you were flying. He had a huge, ancient oak desk by an arched window which stood open, and an occasional breeze rustled the papers he had there.

There was a cold fireplace that tinged the air with soot. There were old couches, cracked and worn, which anywhere else might have looked ancient themselves, but here, in this setting, they looked merely a century old, not a full millennium.

He sat at his desk, reading a file, and looked up as I stepped out of the elevator. He smiled and gestured to the chair opposite him, across the great expanse of millennial oak. As I sat, he said, "The British, with that aggressive genius they inherited from the Vikings, created the empire where the sun never set. They sat on their little island, churning out black smoke, consumer goods, and the best army on the planet. And as they furiously manufactured, they turned their expanding capitalist world into a bloated consumer world. Mind you," he laughed, "by that time, they had passed the baton to the Americans, who really led us into the consumer world, with Coca-Cola, Levi jeans and Ford motor cars."

"I think I've had about as much crazy philosophy as I can handle for this week, Humberto."

He looked a little disdainful. "Really? It isn't crazy philosophy. I need you to understand what it is you are about to do."

"Can you do that *and* make it brief and to the point?"

He stood and turned to look out of his open window. He was big enough to block out most of the light that came through it.

"The consumer age is coming to an end. Power—" He held out his left hand and moved it slowly to the right as he talked. "Power moved from the manufacturer to the worker, via the unions, and finally to the consumer. So that the world by degrees became this grotesque, proletarian feeding frenzy. So that you can now barely go to a restaurant or indeed on a cruise, without encountering these lumpen creatures who can neither speak nor read their own language. Each of these legged-worms must be supplied with what they crave, *whatever* that may be, and have it supplied *instantly!*"

"Humberto?"

He turned his head to look at me, and there was contempt in his eyes. He held my gaze for a moment and then turned back to the window.

"But the age of the consumer is coming to an end. We needed them to consume what we made, and we made too much and too many of everything, including the consumers themselves. In two years, there will be more than the planet can cope with, and in any case, we no longer need them."

"I got all this last night before I passed out. What

do you want me to do?"

"You are not interested?"

"Yeah, sure. Of course I am also traumatized. My entire world has been turned on its head, and I have just killed a man for no particular reason and, thanks to your freezine, I felt absolutely nothing as I did it. Maybe I will come to embrace this as a good thing, in a week or two, but right now I couldn't give a damn that you plan to wipe out all the small guys, turn about eight million of them into an AI hive to be your slaves, and that the point zero one percent of us that have exceptional consciousness will live like princes. So spare me the philosophy and tell me what the hell I have to do."

He narrowed his eyes. "I am not sure whether I admire you or despise you."

"You'd be wise to do both. I won't ask again. I am five seconds from getting in my Range Rover and going home."

He sighed heavily and returned to his seat. It wasn't hard to see he was counting to six.

"In my safe, concealed in the wall behind you, there is an attaché case. Inside it, there are three vials. Each one contains plasma, and within the plasma a single cell. We call it a virus because in many ways it behaves like a virus, but in reality, it is a single-cell biological computer. You will take this case to London, and you will release—or should I say *unleash*—this virus in three very particular places. Then you will travel to Brussels, where we shall meet up, and from there we will travel to Chile."

"Brussels." I nodded. "You are going to release three more in Brussels because it is the heart of the European Union. People travel to and from there from all over the federation. Which means you have at least one other man, traveling to New York, from which it will spread all over the American continent, north, mid, and south."

"Very good."

"But why Chile?"

He drew breath, hesitated, then smiled and shook his head. "One step at a time. When we meet in Brussels, I will tell you. Meantime, follow my instructions to the letter, and we will be the happiest bunnies since the Garden of Eden."

"All right, when?"

"At dawn. You will fly in my private jet from Les Pujols. Sandy will take you this afternoon to the hotel Chateau de Longpre. I have a suite there. You will dine in a way befitting a hero, and in the morning, you will fly to London. I will provide you with official European Commission documents so that you and the case are covered by diplomatic privilege. We do not want a repeat of what happened to Sean."

"Okay, that's good. So where do I release these cells?"

"You have a room reserved at the Savoy. Once there, you will be visited by one of my London associates. She will tell you exactly what to do."

"Will she be as crazy as you? Is everyone in your organization out of their mind?"

For a moment, I thought maybe I had gone too far, but he laughed and said simply, "I hope so. Don't hang on to your sanity too long, Arthur. You may become undesirable."

He stood and crossed the room. I was aware I could have killed him at any moment, and with my inhibitions at practically zero, I had a strong impulse to pull the Sig and blow his brains out. Or better still, to grab him by the scruff of his neck and the seat of his pants and throw him out the window. But I was aware that, though that might have worked six months earlier, this thing had acquired a life of its own, and killing him would achieve nothing right now but to put everybody else on red alert.

It was as Gallin had said: I had to play along and seize the opportunity when it came.

If it came.

He had opened a panel in the wall and revealed a large steel safe. He punched in a series of numbers and letters which I did not catch, and the door swung open. From the dark cavity, he withdrew a black attaché case and handed it to me.

"It is made of two-millimeter-thick steel. The locks are titanium. Any violent act or violent change in temperature will cause the locks to detonate a charge of intense heat that will solder them shut. If the body should then be breached, another smaller charge will be detonated, releasing the virus into the atmosphere. I will be instantly alerted, and I shall take your lovely wife as my own wife and unleash my darkest passions on her. Spoils to the winner."

I took the case. "I don't know if you understand this, Humberto. Maybe I haven't made myself clear. I want this. I want it. It is just a lot to take in so fast on such short notice. Yesterday morning, I had a completely different vision of my life."

He grunted. "Yesterday morning, you were living a fantasy. Surrender to the drug, Arthur. Without it, this is too traumatic. We, the brotherhood, have been living this for years. We are mentally free of the social illusion, and now we finally reach the climax. But for someone like you, still trapped by your conditioning, it is too far beyond your experience of reality. Sandy will give you some doses to take today and tonight. You will enjoy your time with her. She likes you."

I scowled. "Listen, I know in France everyone is really open-minded and—"

"Nobody is going to touch Anne. It is our code that we respect a man's property, and a woman is no less than that. However, the male animal needs to spread his seed. It is a powerful part of what we are. Enjoy Sandy. No one will hold it against you."

He gestured toward the elevator. I hesitated a moment, then turned to go. As the door slid open, he called to me, "Arthur—"

I turned. "Yeah."

"You need to let go of your moral chains. They are not bound to you. You are gripping them. Let go. Enjoy. Be joyful in all the bounty you are receiving. Use the freezine. It will help."

I nodded and stepped into the elevator.

When I stepped out into the vast hall, I pulled my cell and called Gallin. She answered immediately.

"Hey sweetheart. Did you clear everything up?"

"Yeah, it's all good. Listen, I have to fly to London tomorrow morning. We're going down to Les Pujols airport now. So I won't see you for a couple of days."

As I spoke, I saw Sandy move into the doorway across the hall. She leaned on the jamb, watching me and smiling. Gallin was saying, "We? Is Humberto going with you?"

I smiled. "No, Sandy is going to brief me at the hotel."

I heard Gallin laugh. "Brief you or debrief you?"

"That's funny. I'm laughing."

"I'll be waiting for you when you get back, lover boy."

"Love you, kiddo."

I hung up. Sandy and I stood a moment looking at each other across the great, echoing hall. After a moment, she said, "Are you ready?"

"Ready as I'll ever be."

She shook her head. "Oh, no. When I am finished with you, you will be as ready as you'll ever be. I am going to show you parts of yourself tonight you had no idea even existed. You are a glorious monster, Alfred Beaumont. You just don't know it yet." She crossed the room. Her heels echoed on the stone floor. She stopped a couple of feet from me and opened her hand. There was a red plastic capsule in her palm.

"You can see this through, Arthur. You can do what you have to do and bring yourself and Anne to a new world, a paradise on Earth. But first you have to break free from your own mind, from your limitations, your conditioning, fears, and prejudices." She smiled. It was a promise unspoken on her lips and in her eyes. "You could do that by Buddhist meditation, but it might take a thousand incarnations, and we need you by tomorrow morning. So you and me, we are going to do it the fun way. We are going to take a ride."

"We are?"

She nodded. "It could get wild, so unfasten your seat belt, big guy."

What happened over the next eighteen hours is faithfully recorded in my unpublished memoirs, which will remain unpublished until after my death. What I can tell you is that it did get wild, and I did unfasten my seat belt. You sign up for a job like ODIN, you know from time to time you're going to have to make sacrifices.

By ten a.m. the next morning, I was standing within the small departure lounge of Les Pujols airport. I was aware of a slight distortion to my sense of perspective, so that at times everything, however far away, seemed to be right there in front of me. The blue of the sky outside was of an extraordinary intensity; and Sandy's beauty, her smell of roses and jasmine, the sound of her voice when I looked at her, it all seemed to fill the whole of my experience. She took hold of my face and looked right into my soul.

"You are a god, Arthur," she told me. "Do you understand that?"

"Yes," I told her back. "I have understood that completely tonight."

"You are going to take an action tonight which is going to change all of reality, all of history. You are going to bring down the princes and rise up on your own throne. You know that, in your bones, in your soul, don't you?"

"Yes."

She smiled and stroked my cheek. Her face radiated the deepest love. "Who is your goddess, Arthur?"

"You are. You are my goddess."

"Fly," she said, "fly to your destiny."

I walked through security. I knew I had been given a hallucinogen. I was struggling to care because whatever it was, it was triggering truckloads of dopamine into my bloodstream, and I was on cloud nine. She had not been kidding. I was a god, and reality was so damned plastic I could do what I liked with it.

After takeoff, I slept, which was probably just as well because the state I was in I might well have tried to fly ahead of the plane. By the time we touched down at City Airport in London, I had come down from cloud nine to the somewhat more peaceful seventh heaven, and my brain had started working, if not perfectly, at least well enough to make a little bit of sense of things. I no longer believed I was a god, for example. I was just very like one.

There was a driver there to meet me. He had a large, dark blue Audi and made sure my attaché case and I were safely in the back before he locked us in. Then we drove in silence through the city. My sense of perspective had settled to near normality, and the intensity of colors and sounds had also settled somewhat. I still found it hard to care about anything much and felt a pleasurable sense of overpowering superiority. The fact that I had been locked in the back of the car didn't alter that sense of superiority.

I am pretty sure, in retrospect, that the effect of the drugs they had given me would probably have pushed me over into psychosis if I had not hit on the trick of observing all of those weird phenomena and crazy feelings from a kind of neutral spot, as though I was a scientist watching an experiment from a detached location. It was like the day-to-day me had become this complete asshole, and I, the real I, was watching from above. If it had not been for that trick of my mind, I don't know what I might have done. Because basically, I was crazy, and I didn't care.

The driver checked me in and saw me up to my suite. There he told me in a thick, East European accent, "Sleep now. Woman will come with instructions."

I turned to him as he reached the door. "Watch your manners, slime ball. You're talking to a god, remember?"

He let his eyes do the talking, gave me a once-over, and left.

What I really wanted was to sleep twelve hours. But the detached scientist in my head noted with interest that there was another desire, one that came from somewhere else, from some deep, secret place, that drove me to do what I did next.

I took the elevator down to the lobby and walked out the main door to the taxi rank. I gave the driver fifty pounds sterling and told him, "This is like the movies. I think somebody might be following me. Just drive around for ten minutes and see if we have a tail. If we haven't, take me to any big shopping mall."

"Right you are, sir. But I'll have to charge you what's on the meter."

"No problem."

Nobody knows the streets of London like the cabbies. They call it "The Knowledge," and it is almost mystical. This guy weaved, snuck, doubled back, nipped and tucked for ten minutes and told me, "If you still have someone on your tail, sir, they deserve to get you. Shall we go to the mall now?"

I laughed, probably too much, and told him yes.

He drove me to Mega Shopping on Shelton Street, I paid him what was on the meter, on top of the fifty I'd given him, and strode, still godlike, into the mall. It didn't take me long to find the cell phones, and I bought two disposable burners which I took with me to a pub on the upper floor. There I ordered a pint of their best bitter and sat in the corner, where I phoned the office. Lovelock tried to put me through voice recognition, but I told her, "I have no time for that. This is code nine by three red. Put me through."

Half a second later, Nero was on the line.

"Speak."

"Okay, I need to give you some background first, and I have very little time. I am drugged up to my eyeballs, I am as high as a kite, I believe I am a god, and I don't give a damn about anything very much. I am making this call because I am clinging to reality by my fingernails. Got that?"

"Yes. Where are you?"

"Mega Shopping Mall, Shelton Street, London. I have been given a mega dose of something they call freezine, which breaks down your inhibitions and boosts your dopamine, and I have to tell you it is *good!*"

"Stop it."

"Okay, so I am booked into the Savoy. I have three viruses in an attaché case. Later this afternoon, a woman will bring me instructions on where and when to release them. They have Gallin."

"What do you know about the virus?"

"It's not a virus. It's a unicellular biochip with a program written in protein by a photon laser. It is AI on steroids and is going to take out well over ninety percent of humanity. They are going to be released in London, Brussels, and New York. I am going to be a prince in the new Eden."

"Alex, get a grip. You know that is a lie."

"Yeah, I know," I sighed, "but it is so hard to care."

"You are speaking from a burner?"

"Of course. I will toss this one, and then I have

another."

"Why are they leaving you unsupervised? That doesn't make sense."

"Because they actually *believe* I am an amateur oenologist who has a military background and is in love with his wife. They have no idea I am really James Bond."

"Get back to your hotel. Try to sleep this off. Get a grip. We'll be in touch."

"Sir?"

"What?"

"Are you married and called Mr. Green?"

"Of course not! And don't be impertinent!"

I smiled and hung up. I snapped the SIM card, dumped the phone, and made my way back to the hotel.

THIRTEEN

I t was a ten-minute walk via Long Acre and James Street. I strolled with my hands in my pockets, enjoying the occasional sunshine and that peculiar smell of diesel, chocolate, and tobacco which for me defines London.

I was confused, but my drug-induced lack of concern, ironically, gave me a certain amount of clarity. For example, I knew I was on borrowed time, and so was Gallin. I knew I was being played, and I knew that, though right now Humberto and Sandy didn't realize who we were, it was a matter of very little time before they found out. I could also see clearly that not giving a damn and focusing on the million tiny pleasures of being a god walking down an old London road in the dappled, patchy sunlight was a serious problem.

It was a serious problem I was going to have to address, just as soon as I got back to the hotel, stretched out on the bed, and called room service. I chuckled. Wasn't that what everybody kept telling me to do? Relax and get some sleep?

I ambled into the hotel, rode the elevator to my suite, and stood under a cold shower for fifteen minutes. After the initial shock, it was enjoyable and slowly began to ground me a little.

When I stepped out of the shower and started drying myself, I heard a tap at the door. I pulled on my pants and opened up. It was my driver from the airport.

"What do you want?"

"We need talk."

"You need to talk."

"No, you need."

It seemed convincing, so I stepped back and let him in. He followed me into the sitting room. I jerked my chin at him. "So talk. What do you want?"

"You go to shopping mall. You buy disposable mobile telephone. You make call."

"So what?"

"Who you call?"

"Mind your own damn business."

"I not tell anyone yet. I tell da Silva and he kill you."

"So this is blackmail."

"*Da.*"

"How much do you want?"

"Ten thousand."

"When is this woman coming?"

"We have time." He checked his watch. "One hour still."

"Make it twenty."

Nothing changed on his face. East Europeans were back of the line with the Chinese when facial expressions were being handed out. With Eastern Europe, it's either really joyful or bottomless despair. Anything in between is just an expressionless stare. But he did seem more alert.

"Why more?"

"For ten grand you keep your mouth shut. For another ten, you give me information."

"What information?"

"Let's start with how you knew I went to the mall."

"Your shoes."

"There's a bug in my shoes?" He nodded. "Any other bugs?"

"No. Shoes."

"You're Russian. Are you with the Russian mob or do you work only for da Silva?"

He stared at me a moment with a slack jaw. I guess he decided a lie would be too complicated because he shrugged and said, "No. I work for Russian Military Intelligence. You call it GRU. We are cooperating with Commissioner da Silva."

"You are military intelligence, and you share this information with me?"

I sounded incredulous because it was hard to believe, but he just shrugged. "Everything going to hell. I get what I can and try to survive."

"Everything is going to hell how? Why?"

Another shrug. "Is what everyone is telling. Shitstorm end coming. Look what you see. Missiles hit Kremlin. Everybody dying. Enough talk now. Give me my money. I go."

"Fine." I stood, said, "Hold the towel," and shoved it in his face. While his hands were occupied pushing it away, I slipped my right arm under his chin, grabbed my left bicep and slipped my left hand behind his neck. I squeezed, pulled him to his feet and choked the life out of him. When he'd stopped kicking, I lowered him to the floor and broke his neck with my heel, just to be on the safe side. Then I dragged him into the bedroom, took his Glock, his wallet, and his car fob, and shoved him under the bed. After that I opened the balcony, ordered a bottle of Krug in a bucket of ice, along with caviar for two, and dressed to receive a lady.

The champagne and the caviar arrived fifteen minutes later, and fifteen minutes after that, there was another tap at my door. I opened it and smiled.

I stood looking at her and thinking about Gallin. I guess I had spent too long listening to Humberto da Silva philosophize about everything under the sun, because I found myself thinking Gallin was beautiful because she was made as God intended her to be (this from an atheist!), and this woman ought to have been beautiful because she was made the way some team of plastic surgeons thought God wanted a woman to be. Does beauty need a soul? Gallin had a soul. This woman did not.

She smiled like she'd caught me drooling.

"Arthur Beaumont?"

"That's me. Who are you?"

"I am here on behalf of the goat, to explain a few things to you."

I smiled and tried to mean it. "In that case, you are the woman I ordered caviar and champagne for."

"Good, there is no point doing business unless you can mix it with pleasure. Am I right?"

I stood back so she could come in. "Oh, I suspect you get it right all the time." She sashayed past me. As I closed the door, I said, "You got a name or shall I just call you babe?"

She headed for the terrace where the champagne was. "You can call me whatever you like, sugar."

I popped the cork and poured two glasses while she

sat and watched me. When I handed her her glass, our fingers touched, and I told her, "Let's get the instructions out of the way, shall we? Then we can relax. I am new to this damned freezine, and I don't mind telling you, I have about six hundred years of Protestant inhibitions to get through. Any help you can provide would be gratefully accepted."

She laughed her way through most of the speech, and when I had finished, she said, "I'm afraid you're not going to have much time for burning inhibitions today, Arthur. But we can catch up in the next week."

"In Chile?"

"Oh no, I don't get to go to Chile."

"You don't, huh? Well, I say that's a crying shame. So what are my instructions, chief?"

She spooned some caviar onto a cracker and stuck it in her perfect, plastic mouth. She closed her eyes while she chewed, then sipped champagne. When she was done, she reached in her handbag and pulled out a long, white envelope, which she dropped on the table in front of me.

"You have three addresses in there. Appointments have been made with those people personally by Humberto da Silva. He has asked them to meet you because you are to deliver a set of files to them on a USB memory drive. Each drive is contained in a sealed, plastic envelope. You will hand it over, they will plug in the drive and you will kill them, silently. Then you will leave, taking the drive with you. It will have discharged its program instantly."

I was frowning. "But what about the—" I stopped dead, then whispered to myself, "*Jesus...*"

"What's the matter, Arthur? Did reality just drop

out from underneath you?"

"Everything he said—"

"Everything he said was true, only it wasn't. That's what the gods are all about, kiddo."

"How well do you know him?"

She parted her Botox lips and gave me the once-over. "Intimately."

"What's in Chile?"

"Oh no, you don't. If he didn't tell you, then I ain't going to."

I laughed out loud. "Are you being *obedient?*" I asked with heavy sarcasm. "So while I am releasing these three viruses into the London banking and stock exchange system, he is doing the same in Brussels, and some other guy is doing it in New York. There is no mass murder of eight billion people. We are simply talking about the complete collapse of the Western economy. There will be death from starvation and the collapse of the health system and any welfare systems, but nothing like the fantasy birth of a new Eden he had told me about. Just enough for Russia and China to move in and take over."

She pointed at me across the table. "And you get to become one of the mega-rich elite."

I stood and moved around the table so my belly was just inches from her face. I reached down and held her chin. "Come with me to the bedroom. Now."

She stood with difficulty. I grabbed her and slung her over my shoulder. She squealed and giggled. I carried her into the bedroom and threw her on the bed. There I ripped off her clothes while she gasped and laughed. I was searching for a bug or a wire. She wasn't wearing one, which meant the room was bugged.

"Scream," I said. She laughed and started screaming. I kicked off my shoes and pulled off my socks, balled them and stuffed them in her open mouth. I bounced her on her belly, knelt on her while I pulled out my shoelaces and tied her wrists, then did the same with her ankles. After that, I rolled her on her back again and placed the muzzle of the Glock on her belly.

I leaned down and whispered in her ear, "*I am going to take the socks out of your mouth. Give me the smallest problem and I will blow a hole right through your belly and your spine. Understood?*"

She'd stopped laughing. She nodded. "*When I remove it, you will groan and say, 'Baby, do it again.'*"

She nodded again, twice, and I removed the sock. She complied. I asked, still whispering in her ear, "*Where are the bugs?*"

"*The lamp in the living room, the table on the terrace, and my cell, which I had to activate for pillow talk after we came to bed.*" She gave a small shrug. "*I don't like being listened to.*"

"*Who are the targets in New York and Brussels?*"

"*That information is compartmentalized. Only the executor and his contact know that.*"

"*And Humberto.*"

"*Yes, and Humberto.*"

"*At what time?*"

"*In four hours. Are you going to kill me?*"

"*Squeal and scream and I'll let you live.*"

She made a disturbingly believable show while I phoned Nero.

"Are you telephoning me while performing

coitus?"

"Yes. Listen. I have to whisper."

"Good lord!"

I filled him in. He interrupted only once to say, "That woman is inexhaustible."

"Tell me about it!"

"Make her shut up!"

"No. You shut up, and listen! You'd better get someone to come and get this dame. Be discreet. The suite is bugged."

"What are you going to do?"

"I'll tell you from a different location."

The Botox babe was lying on the bed looking exhausted. I stared at her a while without seeing her, then crawled under the bed and pulled out the Russian guy's shoes. They weren't great, but they fit. I put my socks back on and the Russian's shoes. When I was done, I retrieved my next two doses of freezine and gave them to a very happily smiling Botox Babe. I helped her swallow them with a glass of champagne. When she was done, I put another pair of socks in her mouth, retrieved the attaché case, and left with my shoes wrapped in a plastic bag.

She might have been telling the truth about there being no bugs in the bedroom, but I didn't believe it for a moment. The socks would be uncomfortable, but with that much freezine she'd be happy enough while she waited for the guys to arrive.

For my part, I was running out of time fast, and I had no idea of what I was going to do. What made it worse was that as the freezine was wearing off, I was beginning to actually give a damn, and the full reality of what that bastard was preparing was dawning on me.

I took a five-minute walk to Charing Cross Station,

where I took what the Brits call a tube train on the Northern Line, one stop to Leicester Square. There I got off and left the bag with the shoes to go on without me.

Leicester Square is one of the busiest metro stations in London. I hunched into my shoulders, made myself small, and got lost in the crowd. After that, I spent twenty minutes slipping in and out of small, twisting narrow streets, checking no one was tailing me. Then I hailed a cab and told him, "Just drive for now. I need to check some addresses."

I opened the envelope and scanned the three names and addresses. They were all within spitting distance of the Bank of England, at the intersection of Princes Street, Cornhill, and Threadneedle Street.

"Drop me at Bank Underground," I told him, then added to myself, "I'll make my way from there on foot."

And as I said it, my mind was on Gallin, wondering what the hell was happening to her. I pulled out the second burner, which I should have destroyed after calling Nero. I had to risk using it one more time.

FOURTEEN

Gallin sat on the terrace overlooking the Italian gardens. Dappled light played on the terracotta tiles and across the brilliant white linen tablecloth. The table was set for two, and on it, a silver bucket had been filled with ice and held a bottle of Louis Latour Montrachet Grand Cru from 2018. Gallin had laid the tall, hand-cut Bohemian crystal glasses on the ice too.

Across the table from her, sitting in the shade of a tall pine, Sandy was sipping a *Moriles fino* and smiling her unsettlingly calm smile. Gallin was saying, "I have to be honest with you, Sandy, I didn't drink as much as Arthur. I know the drinks were laced with your freezine, and it had a big impact on him." She gave a small laugh. "The jury is still out on how I feel about that. I am not really sure what you've released there. But I was just sipping."

Sandy arched an eyebrow. "It affected you."

"Yeah, I'm not saying it didn't. Don't get me wrong. I was riding high and having a lot of fun. Hell, *you* know that. You were spying on us. What I'm saying is, it didn't affect me as much as it affected Art."

Sandy took a sip and licked her lips. "A very small amount, Anne, is enough to have a profound effect. So what stopped it having such a deep impact on you, do you think?"

Gallin shrugged. She smiled at Ferrer's wife, who came out laden with a large terracotta bowl of avocado salad with tuna fish, fresh tomatoes, cucumber, sweet corn, and yellow peppers. Behind her, Ferrer had a basket of freshly baked baguettes and a bottle of Spanish olive oil from Baena.

"I have no idea, Sandy, but listen, as it wears off, that whole crazy cult organizing the end of the world thing?" She shook her head. "It's bullshit. Humberto is big and charismatic and a lot of fun. But the bottom line is you are playing with our minds because you're on some kind of ego trip." She watched Sandy's smile broaden to a grin and went on, "What are you doing to Arthur right now? I'm not jealous. I know you slept with him last night, and right now, he's probably recovering from some orgy ritual to Baphomet. That's fine. He'll be okay. But don't hurt him, Sandy."

"Believe me, we didn't sleep. Yes, I spent the night with him, and yes, we had some deep, mind-expanding experiences. I'd like to do the same with you sometime. But there was no orgy ritual to Baphomet. He has simply been given a task to do. Then we will all meet in Brussels and—" She paused. "Well, what happens after that, we'll see. We have no plans to hurt Arthur, Anne. We consider you both a real find. You are us."

Ferrer's wife served them salad while Ferrer uncorked the wine and poured. Then they both bustled away. Gallin sipped and regarded Sandy with an arched brow.

"Thanks, I'll take a rain check. But you can see, just looking at me and talking to me, you can see I am not like Arthur. Arthur is a dreamer. He's got his boots on the ground, but his head is up in the clouds. You offer him a new world with no factories, no overpopulation, with open expanses where a man can have adventures and test himself, and Arthur is yours. Not me. And I am going to tell you again, your unicellular biochip that is going to wipe out mankind is bullshit. Before we go having deep, mind-expanding experiences, you're going to have to tell me what you are *really* about."

Sandy drew breath, but Gallin leaned forward and held her hand.

"Hey, listen. You are both loaded, big time, so whatever you're about, I am happy to be a part of, and the freezine is a gas, especially if there are really no side effects. But I want the truth. I have too much ego to be playing a supporting role in somebody else's game."

Sandy had been eating delicately while Gallin spoke. Now she put down her fork, patted her lips with her napkin, and sat back, sipping her wine. After a moment, she said, "I would not expect anything less from you. Shall I tell you why the freezine had less of an impact on you? Because there was less to liberate. It tore down the structure of Arthur's worldview and sense of reality because it was a false structure. But you? You can already see what is real and what is false. So all it did for you was to give you a kick."

"Maybe. I can certainly see what's false. I can also smell it."

"But to tell you everything?" She shook her head. "Apart from anything else, there is just too much to tell at one sitting. What Humberto has created here is vast, more than you can imagine. And yes, you re right, it is protected by ring after ring of smoke, mirrors, and lies. And the freezine helps." She threw back her head and laughed out loud. "The president of France believes there will be a European war triggered by Brexit, and in the ensuing chaos, he will rise to be the Emperor of Europe!" She laughed some more while Gallin smiled and watched her. "The Pope believes that aliens are coming from Zeta Reticuli and the Vatican will be the church through which they control humanity. If I told you all the fantasies Humberto has cultivated in the high offices of power around the world—"

"I would probably believe you. The president of France comes as no surprise."

"Keep in mind, Anne, that the people who rise high in politics are generally unbalanced and overambitious. You need to be to get there. Feed them the right fantasy, the one that feeds their bloated egos, the one they really need to believe, support it with a big dose of freezine, and they will go with it. Hitler and Stalin are the models to follow here."

Gallin grunted, chewed, and watched. Sandy went on.

"Anyhow, you're right. We are not about to wipe out over nine-tenths of the human race, much as we would like to. The planet will take care of that herself before the second decade is out. What we are going to do is effect a violent shift in the balance of power, and in doing so, we will consolidate the power of the Brotherhood globally, and the individual power of certain key members. Humberto has taken a real shine to Arthur, and I, personally, would really like you with me."

"With you?"

She nodded. "Yes."

"What does that mean? I'm straight, and I love my husband."

Sandy leaned back in her chair and gave another pretty laugh.

"Anne, I love that you are straight and love your husband. He is a very lovable man with a lot of inner fire. I don't blame you. But beasts like Arthur and Humberto need women like us to fan their flames. That you are straight and in love does not mean that we cannot be close. Does it?"

Gallin was about to ask her to define close. Instead, she smiled and made a show of relaxing. "No, of course not. And I would like that too."

Sandy picked up the bottle and refilled their glasses.

"What do you say we finish the wine, go down to the pool, take a couple of capsules each, strip off our clothes, and have a swim?"

Gallin laughed. Her cell rang, and as she answered, she said absently, "Sounds like a plan. Yeah, Anne Beaumont."

"Good afternoon, Mrs. Beaumont, this is Alex, your investment broker in London."

"Oh, yes, hello." To Sandy, she said, "Excuse me, I have to take this." She stood and walked away a few steps, saying, "I'm sorry. I didn't recognize the number."

"Oh, yes, I had to change it. So much interference on the other one."

"I see. Any problem?"

"It's a little complex. Have you got a moment?"

"I have a guest, but if we make it brief."

There was a small laugh. "It has been a little mad in the office over the last couple of days, but the aftermath seems to be wearing off. Now, important point, there seems to be an unexpected glitch in the stock exchange software." There was a pause. "What we might have called before a *virus*—"

She gave a small laugh. "I suspected as much."

"You're a smarter cookie than I am."

She said absently and quietly, "Yeah, well, you drink too much." At the other end of the terrace, she could see Sandy reaching in her handbag and pulling out her cell. She said, "Alex, as I said, I have a luncheon guest. I'm going to have to ask you to cut to the chase."

"Yes, of course, forgive me. The thing is, it is nowhere near as bad as we initially thought. However, it is still very bad. We are waiting to see how Brussels and New York respond, but we must assume they will be affected. Still, I mustn't keep you. Perhaps we could talk later."

Sandy was talking on the phone. Gallin said, "I'll call you on this number when I get a chance."

"Super. Daddy knows best."

"Gotcha. Hang up."

She slipped the phone in her pocket and walked back toward the table, speaking loudly.

"My broker in London. Can you beat it? Calling at lunchtime. I told him I have luncheon guests. Cut to the chase."

Sandy watched her approach and said into her cell, "Forget it. We'll talk later."

Gallin sat. She knew the question that was coming: who was her broker in London? She didn't know any brokers in London and was pretty sure Sandy knew them all. There was only one way she could head her off. She smiled and said, "Are we just going to sit here and talk, or are we going to swim?"

* * *

In New York, Mike Chen sat on the sofa in his suite at the Plaza on 5th Avenue. Across the coffee table sat Jane Gray. On the coffee table between them, open, was an attaché case. He was inspecting its contents, what looked like three pen drives, each sealed in a small, transparent cellophane bag.

He closed the case, and the woman handed him a long, white envelope.

"In there you have three addresses in the Financial District. Humberto da Silva has personally made appointments with all three of them. He has arranged for you to meet with them and deliver a set of files contained on a USB flash drive. Each drive, as you have seen, is contained in a sealed, plastic envelope. You will hand it over. They will plug the drive into their computer, and in that instant, you will kill them. Do it silently. Then leave, taking the drive with you. It will have discharged its program the moment it was plugged in."

"Kill them?"

"Kill them. Then fly back to Hong Kong and await instructions."

"Okay, anything else?"

"No."

"Then go."

She stood, thought a moment about suggesting some fun with a dose or two of freezine, but decided she didn't like his mean, pinched face and left instead.

When she was gone, he had a shower and changed his clothes, giving her plenty of time to get away from the hotel. There was no reason anyone should associate her with him, but he was a cautious and meticulous man.

He went down in the elevator, crossed the lobby, and trotted down the red-carpeted steps onto West 59th. He walked a block east toward Madison Avenue before hailing a cab. As he climbed in, he said, "Take me to Broad Street, corner with Exchange Place."

The driver glanced in the mirror and grinned. "On our way, boss. Good day so far?"

Mike Chen pulled out his cell. "We don't need to be friends, driver. Just get me to Broad Street and Exchange."

* * *

At Castèl de Coudrey, a helicopter had landed some half an hour earlier, to transport the commissioner for Directorate 32 to Brussels. He had told the pilot to wait in the kitchen, where he would be fed coffee, brioche, and croissants fresh from the oven. Then he had telephoned to Dr. Hussein Sasani and instructed him to come immediately to his study in the tower.

It was mid-afternoon, and Sandy was back from her visit to Anne Beaumont. He called her and told her to join him and to bring with her the head of security and his two senior lieutenants. He then went to his small silver chest, where he kept his white powder. This was freezine as he took it, pure, not contained in capsules, but by the spoon.

He stirred a measure into a glass of pure mountain spring water and drained it. As it went down, he felt every liquid ripple, his blood surge and every blood vessel vibrate. His mind soared, his perception sharpened beyond imagining, and he roared at the top of his lungs, "*I am God! I am God! I am God!"*

Twenty minutes later, the elevator doors hissed open, and Dr. Hussein Sasani entered, accompanied by Sandy and the three security men. The men took up positions beside the elevator doors, and Humberto approached the doctor with his hands outstretched.

"Doctor, Doctor, Doctor. Allow me to welcome you and commend you on your magnificent work. Your contribution will transform the world we live in, Doctor. We are at the dawn of a new age. We shall move now from the cruel reign of the machine back to the glory of the gods."

"It has been an honor to serve you, my lord."

"I know, I know it has. Sandy, go and sit on the sofa where you will have a good view." He gestured her over and she went and sat. He turned back to the doctor. "My only regret, Hussein, is that your service has come to an end and the Brotherhood has no more use for you."

The doctor bowed and mumbled, "I am always at your service, my lord."

"Yes." Humberto chuckled as he moved to his desk and retrieved a Viking sword some thirty-six inches long with a leather-bound handle. "But as I say, we have no use for you. So your service is of no value. What bonus did I say we would pay you? Five hundred thousand euros?" He came and stood in front of the doctor and turned to look at Sandy, who was chuckling. "Doesn't that seem a lot to you, Sandy, for a man who has lost his value?"

He turned back to the doctor. "In fact, Hussein, not only have you lost your value, not only have you become a liability because you know far too much, but from the very beginning, I have found you repugnant. You are a nasty, slimy slug, and I am going to do to you what I have been longing to do throughout your endless years of research."

The doctor was backing toward the elevator, holding out his hands in a begging gesture. The sword caught him full in the side, making him double up. The second blow was on his back and drove him to his knees. Then it was one savage blow after another until he was no longer a man but just a bloody mess of organic matter that had once had a mind and a soul.

Now his soul was free.

Humberto raised his arms and roared up to the heavens like a man demented. He threw down the sword and turned to his security men. "Take me to Brussels. I have three more men to kill today, before I get drunk." He turned to Sandy. "Do you want to come?"

She smiled and shook her head. "I have work to do here."

"The Beaumont woman. You like her, don't you?"

"I think we could become friends."

"Good. I have hopes for Arthur. He is strong."

Sandy nodded. "So is she. She is still trapped by her morals, though she thinks she is bad. But I think we are close to a liberating experience."

He laughed. "Wonderful. I'll see you in Brussels."

* * *

I sat opposite Mr. Urquhart. Through the window behind him, I could see the gray walls of the Bank of England. His secretary had just brought us a cup of tea each and a plate of cookies. Clearly, the Old England still survived in small, privileged pockets here and there.

"Now," he said, and smiled in a way you could only

describe as affable. He smiled affably. "Commissioner da Silva advised me that you'd be paying us a visit, and I understand you have some files for us."

I nodded and, having sipped my tea, I said, "Indeed."

I snapped the catches on the attaché case and removed the last remaining drive. Then I paused.

"Now, Mr. Urquhart, I am not sure if you are up to date."

"Up to date?"

"Commissioner da Silva is at present in Chile." I smiled. "Up in the Andes."

This time, his smile was regretful rather than affable. "I'm afraid I am not aware of the commissioner's movements. He simply called on our services for this feasibility study on his proposed portfolios."

"Quite. My point is that he cannot be contacted at the moment." I smiled. "There is very poor coverage in the Andes."

"I should imagine so." He had returned to affable. "Shall we need to contact him?"

"I hope not. I am just covering my bases. I have deposited two of these drives with other brokers—" I leaned forward. "I'm not sure if Humberto mentioned that—"

Mr. Urquhart frowned and looked confused. "No, as I say, he merely—"

I handed over the drive and interrupted him with a grin. "Here, do please insert it. It will download very quickly."

He took the drive and inserted it into his computer, then frowned at the screen.

I said,

"It certainly came as a big surprise to your colleagues at United Investments and Newton and Fanshawe when I told them that my instructions were"—I pulled the Glock from under my arm—"to kill you at this juncture. But before I do, I'd like to ask you directly, how well do you know Humberto da Silva, and has he provided you with any freezine?"

Mr. Urquhart went pale and stared at me.

FIFTEEN

We were at a restaurant called the Devil's Change, a stone's throw from the Robert Schumann Roundabout in Brussels, a mere toss of a brick from the monstrous X-shaped pile of glass and steel named Le Berlaymont, where the European Commission is housed. I gazed at it through the shaky, wooden sash window of the restaurant and felt sure one day it would take off and go and destroy planets where it suspected members of the Rebel Alliance were hiding.

Opposite me, Humberto da Silva was staring at his tablet while he sipped beer. I could make out what it was saying, but he placed it on the table for me to see. It was a reporter from the BBC standing outside the Bank of England. He was young and had what the BBC liked to call a regional accent, which meant that nobody but people from his regions would be able to understand him.

"Senior sources at Scotland Yard are saying little at the moment, but it seems there are no leads as yet regarding the mysterious deaths of three leading brokers here in the City, each one not a hundred yards from the Bank of England. The victims have been named as Charles Urquhart, a senior partner at City Brokers, Cyril Hirschfield, also a senior partner, at United Investments, and Bruce Fanshawe at Newton and Fanshawe, and we do know, Kirsten, that the three men were murdered within an hour of each other, in their offices, in a manner police sources have described to me as, and I quote, exquisitely professional."

A disembodied female voice from the studio cut in and asked, "That is a very peculiar way of describing it, Rashid. What did they mean exactly?"

"Well, Kirsten, it is a little gruesome, and more queasy viewers may not want to hear this, but apparently the killer slipped an extremely sharp blade down behind the left collarbone. This not only pierces the heart but also severs the carotid artery and the jugular vein. Death is said to be almost instant, silent and, above all clean because the massive bleeding that ensues is all internal."

By this time, Humberto was laughing not noisily but bigly, wobbling his whole body over the bistro table.

"You are quite a find, my dear Arthur. I am tempted to be suspicious of you. You clearly have a very particular set of skills."

"Yeah, I told you I was in the Army. I also told you it was a set of skills I had hoped to have left behind."

"Bah!" He spread his hands and leaned back as the *garçon* deposited an earthenware dish of snails in front of him. "You will not need to use them again, my dear boy, but continue using the freezine, and I guarantee you will miss them. These are natural appetites for men."

"Sure. When can I see Anne?"

He shrugged and slurped. "Anytime you please. I am not keeping you apart, I hope."

"You said we go from here to—"

"South America, yes."

"So do we meet here, there...?"

"It is entirely up to you. I myself shall take my private jet this afternoon. Sandy will be coming here and then flying on in her own aircraft. I understand she brings Anne with her, and perhaps her intention is to collect you. You are welcome to come with me. You are welcome to wait for them. In either case, we shall rendezvous at Talca. At the Lodge Casa Chueca, where they have a decent cellar and a good chef, before going on to our final destination."

He slurped his last snail into his mouth and waved to the *garçon*, who came and took his plate away. He took a long pull on his beer and watched me over the top of his glass as he did it. As he set the glass down, he sighed and smacked his lips.

"You want to come with me or you want to wait for your wife?"

I was still staring at the monstrous building through the window. I'd told Humberto I had no appetite, like I was going through an emotional crisis, but actually I had had a large hamburger and a couple of beers at the airport.

I shifted my gaze and met his eyes.

"This is probably all boring and old hat to you." He nodded. "But to me..." I trailed off and shrugged. "What I am having the most trouble with is something you said."

"Yes? What did I say that is troubling you?"

"If freezine acts as a disinhibitor—I'm paraphrasing, but I think this is what you meant— if freezine is a disinhibitor, when it removes your inhibitions, what is left is the real you."

"That's correct."

"But then that means that in reality I have no

compassion, no pity, I don't care about other people's suffering..." I shook my head, aware once again that in talking to Humberto, I was expressing to him my true feelings. "That is not somebody I want to be."

The waiter came and set a brazed sirloin steak and a salad in front of him. When the waiter had gone, he spoke as he picked up his knife and fork. "Arthur, you, as an Anglo-Saxon Protestant, as you once described yourself, are a deeply inhibited man. Your inhibitions are not your own, but your mother's, your father's, and the generations who formed the societies from which your parents came. They implanted in you the cultural inhibitions of all your ancestors. Am I wrong?"

I thought about it while he stuffed almost raw meat in his mouth.

"No," I said. "I guess not."

"So," he said as he leaned back and watched the waiter fill his glass with red wine, "these inhibitions which you fear to lose because what is left is not what you want to be"—he drew on his wine—"these inhibitions are not yours. They are an illusion of yourself. When you remove them, after so long, it is like removing a dam that holds back the ocean. The tumult! The chaos! The surge of passions and emotions! They are terrifying, but if you embrace the change like a man, fearlessly, you find as the passions subside and settle, that there is compassion and kindness in you. The difference, my friend, is that you get to choose when you use it. It is not dictated by the hive, but by you."

I sighed and looked out the window again. "You trouble me," I said and was further troubled by the fact that it was true. "I need to come to terms with all this. I need to see Anne and talk to her. Preferably without

Sandy being a part of the conversation."

He spread his hands and shrugged the way Frenchmen do. "That is between you three. I understand from Sandy that they have become very close. I warn you"—he wagged a finger at me and grinned—"do not try to come between a woman and her best friend. You will lose every time!"

He finished his steak and his wine, not so much in silence as without speaking. When he was done, he dabbed his mouth with his napkin, belched, and said, "Come with me. They are not far behind. We will land in Santiago, refuel, and fly on just another two hundred miles to a small airfield on Lake Colbún. From there, we will drive to the hotel. They will be just a few hours behind us. They are getting to know each other. We can do the same, become friends. Maybe I can get you to rise out of this state you are in. Enjoy what the gods are giving you. Be joyful."

I smiled a rueful smile that was not entirely honest, but not entirely dishonest either.

"Okay, I guess I am being a bit of a drag. Okay, let's do this, and you can tell me, or show me, what's in Chile."

"Oh, I will," he said. "I will, and you will be amazed, believe me. Good, let us go to the airport. I believe we are all fueled up."

There is an airport within an airport in Brussels International. It's called the Fast Lane Airport, and basically, if you have a lot of money and you pay up before each flight you get to speed through security and all the inconvenient stuff at lightning speed. Our bags had already been loaded onboard and, half an hour after Humberto had drained his Armagnac and espresso, we were climbing the steps into his private Bombardier Global 7500. And twenty minutes after that, we were hurtling down the runway and surging into a clear blue sky. The flight would take thirteen hours, but the plane was equipped with staff, a dining room, a TV room, and bedrooms. It was all in a tube, but it beat first class on a regular airline.

When we were in the air and I was nursing a martini, I asked him, "So what's in Chile?"

He was stretched out on a sofa sipping a gin and tonic. He took a moment to examine the ice and the lime and answered me with a question of his own.

"What is reality, Arthur?"

"Jesus Christ, Humberto! Can't you give a straight answer to any question? I ask you, what's in Chile? You could answer 'a lab,' you could say 'the head office of our operation,' but no. Not only do you answer with another question, which is a pain in the ass of itself, you ask, 'What is reality?' I'll tell you what reality is, Humberto. Reality is that you are a pain in the ass. Now, once again, why are we going to Chile?"

He gave an indulgent, pain in the ass chuckle.

"Arthur, you have a long way to go. You ask your friend Bob or Sam, what have you done this morning and they might answer, 'Oh, I cleaned my car, took out the trash,' but what do you think God would answer to that same question?"

I sighed. "Forget it. I'll find out when we get there."

"Let me explain."

"No, not if it's going to be another pain in the ass lecture about the nature of reality."

"What I do, Arthur, in this world is to create

fantasies for people to experience and live through."

"Yeah, I kind of got that."

"This is why I asked you what is reality. Before you tell me to go and screw myself, or whatever vulgarity you had planned, tell me this. If you were hit by a bus and did not experience it, what would happen?"

"Humberto, that is a really stupid question."

"Think about it."

"I'd become strawberry jelly, but I wouldn't know it."

He sighed heavily. "Am I wasting my time? I do try with you, Arthur. Make an effort." He swung his legs off the sofa and put his elbows on his knees. "If you were crushed by the bus, you would experience it. Being crushed *is* the experience."

"So what's your point?"

"My point, which seems to be wasted on you, is that reality is not that solid rock we believe it to be. Reality is plastic. Because reality is *simply* and *exclusively* what you experience."

I frowned. "Well, isn't that obvious."

He closed his eyes and shook his head. "No, Arthur. I am *not* saying that what you experience is reality. I am saying the opposite. I am saying that reality is *created* by your experience. When you experience something, it *becomes* reality."

I puffed out my cheeks and blew. After a moment, I did a lot of nodding and shrugging. "Look, okay, I grant you it is an interesting idea. But it's one of those things like subjectivism and existentialism. In the end, what difference does it make? However you explain it, we are still living in the same world."

"Are we?"

"Yes."

"Today, you and I and Mike Chen planted between us nine computer viruses that between them will bring down the Western economy. The reality we experience will never be the same again."

"Or is that another fantasy? I don't see the markets collapsing about me."

He shrugged. "It could be, but it's not. Of course the cells will require some time to take effect. Right now, they are learning. But beside that, we need time to occupy our new positions."

"And that's why we are going to Chile?"

"Partly."

"So once again, what is in Chile?"

"You see, let us suppose that you are *not* an amateur oenologist who has made a lot of money from agricultural software."

He paused. I narrowed my eyes but stopped short of answering.

"Let us assume instead that you work for some American state agency, like the CIA. If I had told you the truth from the start, where would we be now? But instead of that, I pumped you full of a wonderful drug that messed with your notion of reality, and I exposed you to people and situations that were ever more bizarre. So where was your attention focused?"

"I don't know. You tell me."

He leaned forward, grinning, shaking his head. "On *your experience!* For you, all of reality was being turned upside down. So any messages or communication you might have had with some head office in Washington would have sent them completely on the wrong scent, if they had paid any attention to you in the first place. It was all too bizarre." He laughed. "And by the time you actually cottoned on to what was really happening, it was too late. Your darling wife was not only at risk of being seduced by the irresistible combination of freezine and Sandy, but you had seen yourself that her life was very much at risk too. Your fantasy, managed by me."

"Son of a gun."

"Quite."

"I am not CIA."

He shrugged and laughed again. "It really doesn't matter. When you see what has become of the Western world by the time we reach our hotel, and when you see what awaits you on the far side, the CIA will have ceased to exist for you. Whether you work for them or not."

We flew in silence for a while, with the black Atlantic moving slowly past beneath us. Eventually I frowned and looked at him where he sat on the sofa, watching me, with his elbows still on his knees.

"So I am going to ask you one final time, and if you don't answer me, I think I might pick you up by the seat of your pants and throw all four hundred pounds of you out of the plane."

"You think you are able?"

"Let's find out."

"Perhaps, when we get there. I am a skilled swordsman, and immensely strong."

"Get where?"

"Headquarters. I own an old monastery in the Maulé region of Chile. It's up in the Andes, on the volcano Quizapú. It sits on the banks of an exquisite lake called *La*

Laguna de la Invernada, the lagoon of the wintered one."

"Headquarters. Headquarters of what?"

"Why, the Brotherhood of the Goat, of course." He laughed out loud. "Arthur, I take freezine by the spoonful. I am totally liberated. I have no inhibitions at all. I am driven wholly by my desires. Bringing down the economy of the West is merely the first step. I have far greater things to do. And I will do them from my headquarters. My advice to you, Arthur, is to get with the program before you start getting on my nerves."

SIXTEEN

ome hours earlier, when Sandy had arrived in her Aston Martin DBS Superleggera Volante with the hood down, Gallin had met her on the steps and told her, "I thought we could have a champagne breakfast before we head off. Is that okay?"

Sandy had smiled and whispered in her ear, "*Let me tell you a secret. Everything and anything is okay.*"

They had both laughed. "That is going to take a little bit of getting used to. Not a lot, but a bit."

"You'll be amazed how quickly you can adapt to luxury and power."

Gallin linked her arm through Sandy's and led her toward the sweeping marble stairs that led to the second floor.

"I thought we could have breakfast in my suite and you can help me pack. How long are we going to be in Chile?"

"Honest truth?"

Gallin giggled and gave her arm a little squeeze. "Always, please."

"I don't know. Things are going to change a bit, and it's hard to predict exactly how. But if you see we have to stay there some time, you can have things sent over, or just buy more over there."

"In Chile?"

They had reached the second-floor landing, and Sandy stopped Gallin and put her hands on her shoulders. "Hey, listen to me. It's a short-term inconvenience as a pretty small price for more power and privilege than you ever dreamed possible. You're giving up Paris and London, I'm giving up Los Angeles, Beverly Hills, Hollywood."

"Okay, point taken. Come on, I'm taking a trunk and hand luggage. You can help me choose."

Sandy sat in a three-hundred-year-old chair by the tall, shuttered window near the foot of the huge four-poster bed, while Ferrer and his wife set a small, fold-down table with smoked salmon, rye toast, whole-wheat crackers, eggs stuffed with salmon and tuna, and a bottle of the ever-present Krug in a bucket of ice.

Gallin had a wooden trunk, reminiscent of a pirate's chest, open on the floor and was making her way through everything in her walk-in wardrobe, asking Sandy for her opinion on every dress, every evening dress, every hat, and every scarf.

"I mean, we will dine out, won't we? It's not *that* remote, is it?"

"Of course we will, my darling."

Gallin flashed her a smile. "You don't want to let Arthur hear you call me that. He'll get totally the wrong idea!"

She laughed like she'd said something hysterical. Sandy watched her and smiled. She whipped out a violet satin bra and panties and waved them at Sandy. "I'm taking these. Arthur hasn't seen them yet. Come on, let's have breakfast. That champagne is going to freeze!"

They sat at the folding table. Sandy shook out her napkin, and as she laid it on her lap, she said,

"It's a sixteenth-century monastery on the edge of a lake. Access is either by mule or by helicopter. There is a village and a road that follows the river Maule down to the coast. But the village and the road are about ten miles away, down the side of a volcano."

Gallin stopped chewing and stared. "Oh—"

"But the house is breathtaking, we have lots of extremely servile staff, and we regularly take the chopper down to Talca, or even Santiago. And it is in the heart of Chile's wine region, so you should be very happy there."

Gallin started chewing again, swallowed, and arched an eyebrow.

"You're talking like we were all going to settle there like one big, happy family."

Sandy helped herself to a stuffed egg. "Would that be so awful?"

Gallin was serious for a long moment, carefully laying a slice of salmon on a slice of pumpernickel.

"I don't know," she said suddenly. "It might be a disaster. I'm not sure how much of Humberto I could take, especially one day after another." She paused, holding Sandy's eye. "Or it might be the best thing that ever happened to me. It all depends how it plays out, right?" She turned her attention back to the salmon and grinned suddenly. "And on how much freezine we have handy!"

She laughed, and Sandy smiled. "We will have an inexhaustible supply of that." She sipped her champagne. "Humberto takes a tablespoon of it at a time. That is partly why he is so"—she paused, watching Gallin's face, then said, "intense. That quantity would knock most people out for a week and probably cause a severe psychotic break. Fun, but not smart. A quarter of a teaspoon keeps me functioning. Anne, I want to ask you a question. Have you taken a capsule today?"

"Is that the question? No, I haven't."

"No." She gave a small laugh. "No, that's not the question. I'd just rather ask you after you'd taken it."

"Come on, Sandy. We're close. It's only been a couple of days, but we've been through more together than most people go through in a lifetime! What's your question?"

"Do you..." She trailed off, then raised her eyes to meet Gallin's. "Do you like me?"

Gallin frowned. "What kind of a question is that? Of course I like you."

Sandy averted her eyes. Her smile was almost bashful. She drew breath and started to speak, but stopped herself.

"What's the matter with you?"

"You'll think I'm stupid."

"Like you give a damn what anyone thinks of you. And anyhow, you're about as stupid as—"

Sandy cut her short. "It's not anyone. It's you. And that's the point. I do care what you think."

"Okay, you are freaking me out. What are you talking about?"

"I don't know. I didn't take a capsule today because I wanted this conversation to be..." She trailed off and shrugged. "To be genuine, I guess. I mean—" She sighed heavily. "With freezine, what expresses itself is the genuine you, that's true. But whatever comes from this

157

conversation, Anne, I want it to be unassisted, with no artificial additives."

Gallin's brows were knitted, and she was staring. "Sandy, what are you saying?"

"I don't know, Gallin. I have never felt this way before."

"*What* way?"

"Jesus, do I need to paint you a picture?" Gallin stared at her plate, then stood abruptly. Sandy said, "I've upset you. I'm a fool. I'm sorry."

Gallin walked away to her trunk and stood staring at its contents, apparently unseeing.
"You haven't upset me. It's a hell of a lot to take in in a couple of days. Forty-eight hours ago, I was staring a new life on a new continent growing grapes and making wine. Now, all this, the drug, Arthur killing that poor man, suddenly going to London, now Chile, and then, on top of it all, this."

"I'm sorry."

Gallin turned away and went to her dressing table. With shaking hands, she opened the top drawer and took out a red capsule. Sandy said, "You have some?"

"From what you gave me yesterday, when you visited. I haven't taken any since then." She popped the capsule in her mouth and washed it down with a glass of champagne. After a moment, she turned and smiled at Sandy. "I think you'd better take one too. You've said what you came to say. Now we need to get over it."

"That bad, huh?"

"No, just a lot to take in. Give me some time." She reached in the drawer again and pulled out a capsule, then handed it to Sandy. "Take it. Let's get laughing again.

Help me pack, and let's get going." Sandy downed the pill. Gallin watched her, and when she'd swallowed, she said, "We have thirteen hours to get through, baby. I hope you've got plenty more where those two came from."

Within ten minutes, they were both laughing again. Sandy was louder and crazier than Gallin had ever seen her, and when she saw that, she urged another capsule on her. Sandy stared, grinning, into her eyes. "It's a lot. It's more than I have ever taken."

Gallin fixed her gaze on her eyes. "Take it. We have thirteen hours, Sandy. I don't want a single inhibition up there. We are going to fly!"

"You're on."

She took another, they called Ferrer to load the trunk into the Range Rover, and she and Gallin took the Aston Martin. Gallin drove. She drove fast and with total control. All the way, Sandy giggled and laughed, or gasped and kept repeating, "Oh, my lord."

At one point, as they were approaching Les Pujols airport, she stared at Gallin and said, "This is like another side of you, aggressive, assertive, powerful..."

Gallin laughed. "Baby, you are going to discover things about me tonight that you never dreamed of."

They parked in the parking lot, were waved through security, and stumbled laughing onto a Bombardier which was an almost identical clone of Humberto's plane. They had a short wait while Gallin's trunk was loaded onboard, and shortly after that, they hurtled, as Humberto's jet would a little later, down the runway and surged into the air before banking south and west. As they cruised out over the dark Atlantic, Gallin reached across the table and held Sandy's hand.

"Is this exciting, or what?"

Sandy observed her with dilated pupils. "I am so excited. This is a new beginning in so many ways, on so many levels."

"I am going to get us a drink."

She stood and went to the stewardess. She found her in a little cabin just before the cockpit and told her, "Fix me a couple of martinis, will you? Say, you always fly for Sandy?"

"This is my first flight. The captain and the pilot are her regular team, though."

"Cool." She returned to their table with the two drinks and set them down. Sandy's eyes were closed. She broke open two capsules and emptied the powder into Sandy's glass. She stirred it and said, "Hey, beautiful—"

Sandy opened her eyes. "You really think I'm beautiful?"

"Inside and out, baby. Drink up, we have a lot of talking to do. By the time we get to Chile, I want to know you like you're my soul mate."

"Anne, that is so beautiful. I think we can be soul mates. I think we can touch the sky as sister souls."

"Right, now I am going deep. You ready?"

"For anything. I am open."

"Have you ever killed a human being?"

"Oh my, right in at the deep end, huh? Not yet. I have watched it done, as you know. Humberto killed the Iranian doctor who created the cell yesterday with a sword. I watched, and it was very powerful. I loved it. When we get to Chile, maybe we could do it together. It would be my first."

Gallin smiled and nodded. "Sounds like a plan, baby. Next, when these cells are released, lots of people are going to suffer, die of hunger, become destitute—"

"Oh, that will be just the beginning—what Humberto has planned is insane. We will become gods. It is the most beautiful dream." She reached for Gallin's hand. "And you and me…"

She trailed off.

"Last question, beautiful, and then you can sleep the sleep of the blessed. This pilot and his second, they okay? They on our team?"

"Totally. Loyal. All good men."

"Great. Close your eyes, beautiful. I'll be right back."

She stood again and returned to the stewardess's cabin. She crooked her finger at her and smiled. She spoke very quietly. "This is not your lucky day."

"Oh, why?"

"Keep your voice down. You ever heard of the Mossad?"

The stewardess, thinking it was a drunken game, dropped her voice. "I think so. Israeli secret service?"

"Right. That's me." She slipped her Sig Sauer from under her arm and showed it to the stewardess. "Now I want you to give me your cell, go to one of the bedrooms and lock yourself in. Do not try to contact anybody, and when we get to Chile, I will put you straight on a flight home. Understood?" Gallin shook her head. "Don't risk your life for people who don't deserve it."

The girl swallowed hard and handed over her cell. Then she retreated toward the sleeping cabins. When she had locked herself in, Gallin opened the cockpit door and shot the pilot and the copilot in the head, aiming down so the slugs would not exit and damage the equipment.

Sandy's voice came to her, giggling. "What was that?"

"Something that is going to make you laugh."

As she said it, she checked that the plane was on automatic pilot. Then she unfastened the pilot's harness and, with great difficulty, dragged him out of his seat and dumped him in the galley. Then she climbed into his seat and dropped the plane to a thousand feet before putting it on autopilot again. Then she released the door.

Immediately, the plane was filled with the howling of rushing air. She slipped out of the seat and moved back toward the main cabin. There, the air was a wild tornado. Their drinks had been sucked off the table and smashed. Sandy was screaming with laughter, covering her face. Gallin grabbed her by the scruff of the neck and dragged her to her feet.

"*What are you doing? This is wild! What are we going to do?*"

She dragged Sandy to the door. Her laughter turned to frantic screams as she tried to push back from the opening. But when Gallin gave her the final shove, the wind did the rest and pulled her bodily through the door, screaming a frantic, horrific scream.

"I told you you were going to fly, soul mate."

She pulled herself back to the cabin and managed to drag the bodies of the pilots to the door and dispose of them too. Then she climbed into the pilot's seat and rose to thirty-five thousand feet and engaged the autopilot.

Finally, she took the microphone and spoke into it.

"This is your captain speaking. Would the airhostess please come to the cockpit? The captain is in need of some coffee and a couple of sandwiches."

She had the cockpit door open, and after a moment

she heard the sleeping quarters door open, and after a moment close. A moment later she was aware of the airhostess's presence just behind her. She said in a trembling voice, "Where is everybody?"

Gallin glanced at her. "They had urgent business in hell. I am going to need some help on this flight. Can I rely on you to help me? I'm pretty sure you don't want to spend the next thirteen hours locked up in a cabin. And in any case, I am with the good guys. Easiest if you just accept that, right?"

She didn't answer for five long seconds. Then she said, "I guess so."

"Good, so some coffee and a couple of sandwiches, and maybe you can clean up that mess in the cabin."

SEVENTEEN

Mike Chen was standing opposite Tiffany & Co. He walked past the main entrance to the Trump Building. He could not remember a time in his life when he had felt fear. It was an emotion he did not understand. It aroused contempt in him when he saw it in others. Yet today, as he had approached the massive, neo-neoclassical edifice, as he had made for the glass and brass doors, fear had twisted inside him like a serpent in his gut, and he had been physically unable to walk through the door.

His mind raced, scanning his motivations, searching for a pattern or a logic that would explain his irrational behavior. He gazed west along the street and saw the tall, sinister spire of Trinity Church rising over Wall Street, lowering down at him. Somewhere in his mind, a voice asked if his conscience feared punishment for his betrayal. But he knew he had no conscience, there was no god to punish him, and where there is no allegiance, there can be no betrayal.

He turned back toward the temple-like entrance and felt sick. This, he told himself, was why AI would soon replace humanity. It did not doubt, it did not fear, and it was never irrational.

Twenty years, he told himself as he pushed

through the door, maybe as little as ten and his company would be implanting AI into human brains. He smiled as he headed for the elevators. Evolution would be racing to keep up. Humberto da Silva was a jackass, but he was right about one thing. The twenty-first century would see the return of the gods. Humanity .3, master of his own evolution, immortal and with mental abilities undreamed of by Zeus.

The elevator doors slid open. His stomach twisted, and he pushed through the exiting dross, pressed his button, and watched the doors close again. He tried to face his fear, but it shied away from his gaze. Was it intuition? Did he intuit that something bad was going to happen? He did not believe in intuition. The brain was a biological computer. It analyzed potentials. So had his unconscious analyzed a potential danger? Was this attack of fear an attempt by his unconscious to warn him of some unperceived risk?

He entered the reception area of the selected financial institution and gave his name at the reception desk. He was invited to take one of the large, leather seats and told that Mr. Garner would be along in a minute.

He sat and fought to ignore the anxiety in his body. Was it the fact that he would have to kill this man? He had never killed a human being before. Neither had he ever considered it a big deal. He had never considered life any more sacred than the electricity in a light bulb.

"Mr. Chen?"

He looked up. Mr. Garner was tall and slim, in his fifties and exquisitely dressed. He was smiling. Chen stood.

"Yes. Mr. Garner. How do you do?"

Garner gestured toward a corridor behind him.

"Let's have a chat in my office. We were all delighted to receive Mr. da Silva's communication. He is a much respected man in our circles."

Chen forced a smile. "He is quite a character when you know him, believe me."

Garner opened a door onto a large office. It wasn't a corner office, but you could deduce that the occupant was on his way. There was a large dresser with a drinks tray, some comfortable armchairs and a sofa, the desk was large, and the window afforded a view of the Financial District and the Statue of Liberty.

Chen heard the door close behind him. "Drink?"

He wanted to say no and get the damned job over with. He wanted to rush to the can and vomit. But he knew he had to play his victim, give him the small ritual pleasures human society demanded. He smiled.

"Thanks, Scotch."

"On the rocks?"

"I try to stay off them, but I'll take them in whiskey."

They both laughed. Garner handed him his drink and went behind his desk.

"Now, let's have a look at these files of Mr. da Silva's."

Chen sat and snapped open the attaché case. From it, he extracted one of the pen drives and handed it over to Garner. As Garner took it from his fingers, Chen was suddenly acutely aware of the razor-sharp porcelain knife he had strapped to his forearm under his sleeve.

"Do you mind if we lock the door, Mr. Garner? There are many years of research contained in that chip. Its value is incalculable."

Garner smiled. "Of course, I understand. And believe me, we are honored that Mr. da Silva has entrusted us with this research."

Chen had no idea what fantasy da Silva had fed this firm. It made him mad because it created the unnecessary risk that he might say something, anything, that did not jibe with da Silva's story. But that was da Silva all over. Maybe the guy was a genius, but he was chaotic, a pain in the ass, and plain dangerous.

Sooner or later, he would have to go.

Garner had locked the door and sat at his desk again. He buzzed his secretary and said, "Ben, I don't want to be disturbed by anybody for the next half hour, understood?"

"Yes, Mr. Garner."

Chen's belly burned. He was aware his breathing had accelerated. He fought to focus, to become calm. Garber glanced at him, smiled, and slipped the flash drive in the computer. He smiled at the screen and nodded at Chen. Chen's left arm dropped, and he felt for the release with his fingers, ready to drop the ceramic knife.

"We have a small problem."

He heard the words and was astonished to realize he felt relief. "A problem? What kind of problem?"

"We're offline."

"Offline?"

"I'm afraid so. This morning, the whole of Wall Street is offline."

"That's impossible."

"And yet. Here we are. Even the Fed is offline this morning."

Chen laughed. It was not a humorous laugh. "The

Federal Reserve can't be offline! That's absurd!"

Mr. Garner laughed. "Yet when you think of the history of banking and the stock exchange, how long has it been *on* line? How dependent we have become."

Chen's mouth had become dry. He tried to swallow. "How long…"

He trailed off. There was a tap at the door. Garner was still smiling.

"I tell them not to disturb me. Will you excuse me?"

As Garner got up, Chen said, "The chip—"

"It's okay. I'll be right back."

Garner unlocked the door and opened it. There were two men in gray suits. Garner stood back, and the men came inside.

"Mr. Mike Chen?"

"Who are you?"

"Are you Mr. Mike Chen, the CEO of Bio-Gen?"

"Yes. You can't be in here right now. Who are you?"

The nearest one smiled at him. It wasn't a nice smile. "At a guess," he said, "I'd say we're probably your worst nightmare."

EIGHTEEN

We had landed at Colorado Airport, which was little more than a dirt strip in a field half a mile from a small holiday resort on the shores of Colbún Lake. It was cold, as befits a country called Chile. It had been raining, and the sky was gray. There was a guy waiting for us there with an Ineos Grenadier. He was tall and barrel-chested with a hooked nose and a black ponytail down to his ass. His suit was expensive in shiny gray. I figured he had a Glock under his arm and a knife strapped to his calf. He didn't talk, and Humberto didn't acknowledge that he existed beyond letting him get our luggage and open the truck doors for us.

Either Humberto had a biochip in his head which allowed him to communicate telepathically with his driver, or they had an established routine which transcended the need for words. Whichever one it was, he drove us in silence for about half an hour through damp, green landscapes that were strangely reminiscent of Scandinavia. The fields were flat, there was an abundance of trees, and the sky was uniformly gray.

Eventually, we came to a small intersection where a steel gate stood closed in an uneven wall painted yellow at the bottom and white on top. On the white part, somebody had painted *Casa Chueca*. Here and there, the paint had run.

We waited a moment while the gate rolled open, and then we drove into the confines of the kind of place you might retire to if you were a Nazi war criminal with a vast fortune concealed in a Swiss bank. We wound through lush, semi-wild gardens and lawns which lay almost randomly among lodges that seemed to have been transplanted from the Austrian alps. I couldn't decide if it was luxuriously quaint or quaintly luxurious. Either way, it was both of those things, complete with rose gardens, tall chimneys, and gingham curtains.

The driver parked outside the largest of the lodges, and I turned to Humberto. "Is this where you incubated the Boys from Brazil?"

His face told me he was not amused. "Hitler was a fool. All that potential wasted with one poor decision after another."

Mr. Silent opened the door for him. I opened my own door and followed Humberto up the steps of the lodge. There was a woman in an apron at the door. She had platinum pigtails and a big grin. She gave him a little curtsey and me another and showed us into a large, high-ceiling living room with a big fire burning in the grate.

"You must be so tired after such long journey," she said in an accent that could only be German. "What can I get you? Some beer? Some ham, cheese, nice bread?"

"Hilda," he told her. "All of that, my darling. Then leave us. I have much on my mind."

I stood with my back to the fire. Outside, the gray sky had started to drizzle. I watched Humberto settle into a large armchair.

"What's the matter?" I asked him. "I haven't heard

you boom, roar, or laugh expansively for about six hours."

He stared at me like I looked as though I smelt bad. "You have a facetious streak."

"I know. When I was born, the midwife took one look at me and told my mother, 'See if you can get him exchanged. This kid is going to be facetious.'"

He gestured at me with his open hand. I said, "Right there, right? I know. So what's wrong?"

"Nothing I can share with you."

He pulled out his tablet and set it on the coffee table in front of him. I nodded some more, with my hands behind my back.

"You should have heard something by now, right?"

He stared at me for a long moment. "Was it you? Did you do something?"

"That's a stupid question, Humberto, and you know it."

He kept staring, then looked at the screen again and turned up the volume. I could only make out part of what they were saying. I caught Manhattan, Wall Street, and police. He said, "They inserted the drives?" He glanced at me. "In London, they inserted the drives?"

"If they hadn't, I wouldn't have killed them, Humberto, would I?" I gave him a moment then pressed, "What's the problem? You have nine of these damned things being inserted. Surely one of them has to work?"

"They are not fail-safes, Arthur." His voice was tense and growing tenser. "They are inserted at key points to gather information, search for each other, and create a matrix. It is the shared information of the matrix that triggers the full potential of the AI."

So if all nine are not successfully inserted—"

"I don't know! It has never been done before. Wall Street is offline!" He stood and paced. He turned and yelled at me, like it was my fault. "Wall Street is offline! It has been offline for twenty-four hours! The Financial District of New York has been offline for twenty-four hours!" He had become almost shrill. "How can the Financial District be offline for twenty-four hours?"

"I'm pretty sure they have fail-safes."

"Of course they have! But why has my man not been in touch? What steps has he taken? This is…"

He clenched his fist, bit hard on his teeth, and made strange noises from his closed mouth.

The door opened, and Hilda came in with a big, homely tray and an even bigger, homelier smile. There were two tankards of beer and enough cheese and ham sandwiches to feed the eastern front. I winked at her, and she left with pink cheeks.

"Call him. Maybe he tried to get in touch. We were in the air. Maybe he couldn't reach you. Or call Sandy. Maybe he's been in touch with her."

He scowled at me like he was debating whether to hew me in twain or feed me to his pet vultures. "Sandy should be here already."

I frowned. "And Anne?"

"Presumably with Anne."

"So call her." He stared at me for a long time till I finally raised my voice to him and said, "What's the matter with you? Call her!"

He stood and went to the door, leaned out, and called, "*Nelson! Geronimo!*"

A few moments later, the driver with the ponytail came in with another guy in an identical suit. Only this guy had short hair and a big moustache. Humberto sat in front of his tablet and stared at me again. I noticed his cheeks were turning pink. When he spoke, his voice was thick, like it was choked with emotion.

"I invoked you," he said.

"You did what?"

"I invoked you, and you know it. I called for a warrior, and you materialized at my calling."

"You're out of your mind, Humberto, and you need to get a grip."

"If I have invoked you, you *cannot* betray me!"

"I have not betrayed you, Humberto. For crying out loud! How much of that damned powder have you been taking?"

He narrowed his eyes. "Don't try to cloud the issue. You know as well as I do that the freezine disinhibits and gives clarity."

"Maybe it does and maybe it doesn't, but right now, you are not seeing clearly. I existed long before you invoked me, and whatever has happened had nothing to do with me. Get a grip, will you?"

"Stop saying that! I am going to call Sandy. If anything untoward has happened to her, the entire machinery of the Brotherhood will come to bear on you, from Russia to China and Iran."

I pointed to the two guys at the door. "Which are these, China and Iran?"

"You and your stupid jokes. How could I have been so blind?"

He dialed and put it on speaker. It rang. I glanced at the two guys. They were staring at me. They thought they knew what was coming.

Then Gallin's voice came over the phone, laughing. "Humberto? Thank God! We have been trying to contact you! What happened to your phone?"

He snarled, "Where are you? Where is Sandy?"

"*What?* The connection is awful!"

"Where are you?"

"We had a problem. Can you hear me? We had a problem with the electronics and had to land at Constitucion, on the coast."

Humberto was red in the face as he screamed into the phone, "*Where is Sandy?*"

Gallin's voice came back laughing, "Yeah! She sends kisses! I can't hear you real well, but we're okay, and we're on our way. We'll be there in twenty minutes!"

He turned his huge, red face toward me. "What is this? What is she playing at?"

"Humberto, will you cut it out! You just fed nine AI biochips into the world wide web. That has never been done before. Now you are freaking out because you're not getting the results you expected but, hey, apparently you *are* getting results!"

He screwed up his face. "*What?*"

"Correct me if I am wrong, but these damned chips have the ability to think for themselves, right?"

"In a manner of speaking, with experience, yes."

"In a manner of speaking, with time. Well, if I am not mistaken, Humberto, one of the reasons Dr. Geoffrey Hinton left Google was because AI was so unpredictable. So what you would expect the damned things to learn in a week, maybe they learned in fifteen seconds. You don't know. And maybe your big plan to shut down the Western stock markets, to them seemed like a stupid idea, and they think it's better to start by messing with communication systems. You don't know. And maybe, just maybe, their messing with the onboard electronics and communication was part of making the plan invisible to pursuing US military planes. *You don't know!* Because, Humberto, you made a Frankenstein's monster, with the big difference that the monster is smarter than Frankenstein! And you just *don't know* what it's going to do next, how, or why!"

He stood and screamed at me so hard I thought he was going to have a stroke. *"No! No! Noooo!"*

I pointed at him like my finger was a gun. *"You-don't-know!"*

"Nooo!"

"And I'll tell you something else, wiseass, you just walked into one of your own fantasies. You, Mr. da Silva, are having a psychotic break that just happens to be real."

I knew what was coming, and I was ready for it. I had picked up one of the tankards like I was going to drink from it. He whirled to the two guards and screamed at them, *"Mátenlo! Mátenlo! Mátenlo!"* which basically meant *kill him* three times.

When you throw a tankard, or a bottle, you don't want to throw it from the neck or from the handle. That way, it lacks force and precision. You want to throw it like a spear, launched straight and with a little bit of spin for accuracy. I had released the tankard by the time he was on his second *"Mátenlo!"* By the third one, it had struck the moustache painfully on the nose, and I was leaping over the coffee table. The ponytail had his hand in his back pocket, and his ugly face was telling me exactly what he had there: a razor-sharp six-inch blade. If he got it out, I was going to have very serious problems.

Instinctively, he assumed I was going to go for a grapple and try to keep his blade in its sheath. I don't like knives. I know what they can do. So instead of closing and trying to immobilize his arm, as soon as I hit the floor, I took another bound and kicked him real hard in the kneecap.

A good kick to the kneecap can be incapacitating, which was something the ponytail was discovering in that moment. Ideally, I would have gone in for the kill, but I felt the moustache's arm slip around my neck. He was going for the very lock I had used on my Russian driver in London. Once closed, there is damn all you can do about it. So I grabbed his wrist in both my hands and took both feet off the ground. I dropped like a stone, and as my feet hit the floor, I rammed the back of my elbow up into his balls. The noise he made was full of pathos, but I wasn't listening. I had other things on my mind.

For a fraction of a second, my attention was split. Humberto was making a flying exit with his tablet, and Ponytail had his knife out and was enraged by the pain in his knee. And I was squatting. You don't want to be squatting when someone comes at you with a knife. I stood as he staggered forward and kicked him again in his damaged knee. That seemed to stop him, so I did it again, and then again. The fourth time he went down. I stood on his hand and stamped my heel on the back of his neck.

I reached into his jacket and pulled out his Glock. It's always a Glock. I shot his friend with it and ripped open the living-room door. I don't know what I expected to see, but I sure as hell didn't expect to see Hilda holding a double-barreled shotgun and an expression like the Third Reich on a Monday morning. I lunged to my left as the cannon exploded. The noise was deafening, and I felt the heat of the blast tear at my shirt and my jacket. In slow motion, I saw the shotgun leap up in her hands, and her face and her eyes screwed. I ran at her with my ears ringing, grabbed the weapon, and levered it from her hands. Then, as gently as I could, I punched her on the tip of her chin. The rage in her eyes clouded, and she keeled over.

I turned and ran for the door. The moment was surreal. Because the door was open, and there were two men standing there. They were twins in gray suits, with gray hair, hooked noses, and very thin legs.

NINETEEN

"We are here," the one on my left said, "to see Mr. Humberto da Silva."

"You just missed him. He just went out. He is probably in the garden."

The one on my right said, "You must be Arthur Beaumont."

"Yes," I said, as though it were a possibility as yet unproven. "And you? Are you from the…"

I trailed off, hoping they would fill the void. Instead, the one on my right said, "There is a woman on the floor holding a shotgun, and there is a hole in the living-room wall."

I nodded. Nothing came to mind that seemed appropriate. The one on my left crossed the hall and peered into the living room. "And there are two dead men here. Did you kill them, Mr. Beaumont?"

I nodded. "Yes." They waited. "They were trying to kill Humberto. That's why he fled."

"You risked your life to save his?"

"I did."

"That's ironic," said the one still standing in the open front door. "Because he summoned us to kill you and your wife."

I laughed without much humor. "That is ironic," I said. "You're right."

"Where is she?"

"She's on her way."

The one in the doorway said, "You seem to be a dangerous man."

I shrugged. "I wouldn't go that far, but I guess if you try to kill me, I'll probably take at least one of you with me."

We stood in a loose triangle, with both of them staring at me with no expression, and me wondering what the hell I was going to do next.

"Are you human?" I asked suddenly, "or did Humberto make you?"

They frowned at each other, and that was when I shot the one in the living-room doorway. I didn't pause. In fact, I was already running when I pulled the trigger. I collided with Thing One, smashed the Glock into some part of his head, and kept on going, feeling the imminent impact of a scalding, lead slug in my back.

I skidded into the driveway and saw two things: the Chevrolet Spin which had evidently brought the Terrible Twins, and the steel gate, closed. I needed to open both, and I needed to make both move, but that would involve going inside again, and I wasn't going to do that. So I ran instead.

I ran toward the steel gate. It was eight feet tall and had cruel-looking spikes along the top. But beside it was a huge, round urn about four feet high with a palm tree growing out of it. I sprinted, jumped, landed on the spherical plant pot, and lost my footing. I grabbed at the palm, lacerated my hands and cut my face, but managed to drag myself up and grab ahold of the nearest spike.

That was when I heard the two firecrackers. The steel gate rang and the brick wall spat splinters. There were two *phuts* followed by a high-pitched whine as the two slugs passed inches from my head.

I glanced back and saw Thing One staggering onto the drive, holding a bloodstained handkerchief to his head, and behind him Thing Two clutching his chest through a very red shirt. He wasn't dead, but he was on his way. Thing One raised his pistol again. I used the spike for leverage and pulled myself the remaining four feet onto the wall. Which was when I discovered it was topped with broken bottles.

I swore violently as my feet slipped on the glass. I felt sharp edges cut into my calf as I half fell and half jumped, and a hail of hot, molten lead smacked into the wall and gate behind me.

I had no time to check my wounds or feel sorry for myself. It might be a matter of seconds before the gate rolled open and they came after me in the Spin. The thought of being taken down by somebody in a Chevrolet Spin gave me a momentary burst of energy. Let it be a Mustang, a Viper, a Jaguar, or an Aston Martin, but not a Spin—not a twin in a Spin.

The pain in my right leg was excruciating, and I could feel the squelch in my shoe. Behind me, I could hear the gate rattling as it began to roll open. Too late, I realized that my best option would have been to lay an ambush for them as they came out. Ahead of me was a perfectly straight road for about a quarter of a mile, and all around me were flat, damp, green fields.

So this would be my final stand. I turned and faced the vehicle as it emerged from the lodge. I tried to ignore the pain in my leg, in my arm, and in my face and raised my weapon. My plan, my strategy, was simple: empty the magazine through the driver's side of the windshield and hope for the best.

One thing was clear. I had to wait until he was close. The maxim *Don't shoot till you can see the whites of their eyes* applied here. A speeding car and an eighth of an inch waver of your gun, over thirty yards can translate into a shot going wide by five or six feet. I had to wait till he was fifty or sixty feet away. Which, if he was doing thirty miles an hour as he approached, would probably give me somewhat less than a second to unload sixteen rounds.

"You're doing good, Mason," I told myself.

The Spin and I stared at each other for four long seconds. Then it turned right and sped away, inasmuch as a Chevrolet Spin can speed.

So I would live to fight another day. I was not elated by the fact. I looked down at my feet and saw I was standing in a large pool of blood. My leg was badly cut, I had no vehicle, and the nearest human being was not only getting farther away but wanted me dead.

In the distance, I heard the roar of an engine. It was indistinct at first but grew louder fast. It dawned on me that the devious son of a bitch had come around behind me. I spun, but that sent shafts of agony up my right leg, which collapsed under me, and I fell. I could hear the engine screaming as it closed on me. I struggled to my knees, screaming at myself to get to my feet, and shoved the Glock out in front of me as the car screamed to a halt three feet from me.

I wavered, confused. This was not the snout of a Spin I was looking at. The driver's door opened and slammed, and a familiar voice said to me, "Let me always remember you like this, on your knees at my feet."

I clenched my teeth and roared as I forced myself back to my feet.

"Gallin," I said.

"You're an animal," she said and took hold of me. "Lie down here, in the grass."

She produced a knife and tore my trouser leg up the knee.

"Jesus Christ! Who did this to you?"

"Don't ask."

"I'm going to patch this, but we need to get you cleaned up."

"Great. Pour whiskey on it. Humberto is getting away, and we have to go after him."

She stared at me for a long moment. "I don't have any whiskey."

She went to the trunk of her car and came back with a white cotton blouse, a bottle of water, and some ointments. She cleaned the cuts, bandaged them tightly, and helped me into the passenger seat of her car, which I now saw was the new Range Rover Sport.

I climbed in, and she got in beside me.

"Where are we going?" I asked as we pulled away.

"Close your eyes. I'll tell you when we get there."

She drove for a couple of hours, heading east. The pain in my calf was bad. It throbbed and occasionally sent shards of pain through my leg. I opened my eyes at one point and saw that we were passing Lake Colbún, where Humberto and I had landed. Ahead, I could see the Andes rising into the gray clouds.

"Where are we going?" I asked again and closed my

eyes. "That son of a bitch is getting away."

"You going to complain or are you going to try and sleep?"

"I'm going to complain."

"Then if you have to talk, tell me what happened. How come he ran?"

I opened my eyes and shifted my head to look at her. "Gallin, he is seriously out of his mind. I mean, he is really crazy."

"You think?"

"I'm not kidding, Gallin. He is not brilliant and eccentric, you know, like Nero. This guy is out of his mind."

"Yup."

"But—" I paused while an invisible elf drove a knitting needle through my leg. When he was done, I sagged. "How did that guy get to be a commissioner in the European Commission? How did he rise to such a position of wealth and power if he is that crazy?"

"You're really asking?"

I nodded. "Yes."

The lake was gliding past on our right, and the road we were on plowed deep into a ravine where the mountains soared high either side. The drizzle intensified and became a sporadic rattle on the windshield. The wipers squeaked.

"Remember when we met him?" I closed my eyes and nodded. "Okay, so imagine, I mean just for the sake of the argument, imagine we were just a normal couple taking a break in the Pyrenees, dining in that restaurant."

I smiled. "Nice."

"You must be delirious. So we're having dinner and

DAVID ARCHER

this guy walks in. What would we think of him?"

I nodded and shrugged, still with my eyes closed. "Big, bombastic, French... A pain in the ass but entertaining."

"Right, now imagine you are a rich, influential politician, and you meet this guy. Not only is he entertaining, he is also extremely rich and well-connected. What do you do when he invites you to dine at his castle in the mountains?"

I sighed. "You accept."

"And before you know it, your inhibitions have gone over the battlements along with your shorts and your wife's brassiere, and Sergio is busy taking photos. Next morning, he gives you the option, keep enjoying your membership of Europe's most exclusive club or get yourself a box because tomorrow you'll be clearing your desk."

We drove in silence, steadily climbing. On our left, the mountains became more massive, with their peaks lost among the low ceiling of cloud. After a while, she spoke again.

"I think that's how it started. But the quantities of that powder he took. He takes it by the spoonful, and I think that is driving him deep into psychosis."

I turned and looked at her. The lights had come on in the growing gloom, and the dash cast a soft glow on her face.

"What happened to Sandy?"

"She had to fly."

"Oh."

"You liked her?"

"Not really. I always felt there was an ugly person

behind that beautiful exterior."

"There was. She wanted us to be close, and our next bonding session was going to be killing somebody together."

"Sweet Jesus. Is this just now, Gallin? Or have powerful people always been like this?"

She shrugged. "I think they have always been like this, just occasionally you get one, or a group, who are especially crazy. But it's a vicious circle, Mason. Crazy people are drawn to power, and power makes people crazy."

We wound on up through the ravine, following the course of the river upstream on our right, and as evening began to close in, we eventually came to a broadening of the River Valle, till it was maybe a mile across at its widest point, where the ravine forked into two steep canyons.

Here the river ran broad and quiet among white sand and pebbles, and either side of the water, there were cabins and chalets that would have looked at home in Austria or Switzerland.

Gallin pulled off the road into the parking lot of a hotel. She told me to wait, climbed down, and headed for reception. I muttered "Screw that," to myself and began to maneuver myself out of the Range Rover. I stifled several cries of pain and had just managed to slam the door when Gallin emerged with a couple of young fellows in white jackets and bowties. They saw me trying to walk on my own and started to run, crying out, "*No, señor! No!*"

Gallin informed me, "You're an asshole." The guys were kinder and helped me into the hotel reception, talking to me, each other, and Gallin all the way. They deposited me in a large chair, Gallin tipped them excessively, and they went back to the restaurant, where they were waiting on tables.

The receptionist, one of nature's mothers, approached with a hand on either cheek, saying, "*Hoyhoyhoyhoyhoy!*" which I gathered meant something like, "Oh, my!"

"What happen?" she asked me, and then looked to Gallin for an answer.

"He fell. He won't listen to me. I told him not to climb up on the rocks, but he won't listen."

"Men."

"Right? And he slipped and fell. I knew he would. But the worst of it was, there was a broken bottle, and he hit in just such a way—"

She made an illustration where her right hand was my foot and her left hand was a rock with a broken bottle. The woman shook her head and said, "*Hoyhoyhoyhoyhoy!*" again. "I have call the doctor. He is comin' now." She turned to me and said, very loudly in Spanish, "*Hay que tener mucho cuidado!*" I smiled and nodded, and she repeated in the same loud voice, "You got to be very careful!"

"I guess so. Meantime, can I have a strong painkiller and a glass of whiskey?"

Gallin spread her hands and gave the woman a "See what I mean?" look. The woman went away, shaking her head and muttering "*Hoyhoyhoyhoyhoy!*" under her breath.

Gallin told me, "We book into a room for tonight. We eat, and you get some healing done. Tomorrow, we decide what we do over breakfast."

"That man is at large, Gallin. He is more dangerous than we know."

"There is nothing we can do tonight, Mason. When we've got the room and dinner fixed, I am going to call my dad. I suggest you call Nero. Right now, I think they can do more than we can." She pointed at my bare leg, and then at the rest of me. "And look at you. You're a mess. We need to get you some clothes. Where's your luggage? I brought a trunk."

"Yeah, well, it's all at the lodge, and last time I was there, a really cute German hausfrau tried to blow me away with a double-barreled shotgun."

"You just make everybody love you, don't you?"

"You're mean. You shouldn't be mean when I'm in pain."

"Ah, quit griping."

She walked over to reception and was in the process of organizing our room when a man with a black briefcase stepped through the door. He glanced around, caught sight of my leg, and winced.

He approached me and said, "I am doctor."

I smiled and injected some pathos into it. "Good," I said. "I am sick."

"Dr. Jimenez. I look your leg."

"Yes, please, Dr. Jimenez."

TWENTY

T he doctor told Gallin that really, I needed to go to a hospital. There were a couple of gashes that were very deep and needed stitches. She told him she'd pay him a month's wages if he'd take care of it. She also told him she was a military doctor in Israel and she could do any stitching that needed to be done. That didn't convince him, but the month's salary did, so he provided local anesthetic, antiseptic dressings and all the rest of it, and Gallin provided the good-humored ruthlessness which I have grown to love so much in her.

It wasn't the kind of hotel where you get twenty-four-hour room service. It only had three stars, and most of those were just for being so nice. In fact, they were kind enough, in view of my absent wardrobe and damaged calf, to bring our dinner up to the bedroom. Gallin told me that damaged tissue requires a lot of first-class protein, so she ordered salmon and avocado salad and two T-bone steaks big enough to feed a marching army.

"As for the Chilean wine, I know it's good, and I know you want it, but we have a tough day tomorrow, so you'll make do with beer."

She put my appetizer in front of me, handed me a napkin, and poured my beer.

"You do care really, don't you?" I said, milking the pathos as long as I could.

"No." She stuffed some salmon and baguette into her mouth and spoke while she chewed.

"One of the things I did after I landed was to buy half a dozen burners. That's three for you and three for me."

"Good." I held out my hand. "I'll call Nero."

"You'll call Nero, but first you'll eat. Your head's not clear, we need to talk, and you need to stop behaving like a sissy with a broken apron string. Cowboy up. Eat meat. Then we'll talk, and after that, you call Nero."

I chewed, watching her for a bit. "You really are like that, aren't you?"

"Yup. You should see me with a pair of handcuffs." She winked, and we continued to eat in silence.

After the meal, she allowed me a large Bushmills because she said it would be good for my attitude. She helped me to an armchair and put my foot on another chair with a pillow under it. As I sipped, she told me I had better not be a burden to her the following day, and I told her to take a hike. Then I called Nero and put it on speaker.

Lovelock's voice came on the line, but only to a sing-songy, "One moment," and then more quietly, "It's Mason."

"Alex, I am eating a rare beluga caviar. Can it wait?"

"Sure, if you have a portfolio of investments in Chinese IT and AI, and Iranian oil, there is no hurry."

A big sigh through his big nose. "Very well," and then to somebody else, "Put it on ice, but pour me some of the Dom Perignon. Where are you, Alex? Get me up to date."

Gallin stood at the window, shaking her head silently while I put him up to date. He interrupted me just once to say, "Twins?"

"Yes, sir. Identical twins."

"In their fifties, you say? That would put them at about 1970 or '75."

I looked at Gallin and spread my hands. She shook her head in sympathy.

"Yes sir, may I continue?"

"Of course. So you killed one of them?"

"He wasn't dead when I left, but he didn't look great. I think they went to get medical help instead of coming after me."

I finished the story up to arriving at the hotel and calling him, then said, "Sir, Humberto da Silva is out of his mind. I know some of our own presidents have been a bit crazy, but this is on a different scale."

He grunted. "It is a fact, Alex, that people drawn to great political power are often borderline psychotic. That is to say, they sometimes have difficulty distinguishing between reality and fantasy. From what you tell me, this is not only his case, but he fully embraces it and fuels it with this drug, probably some form of benzodiazepine tropane alkaloid. It would be interesting to know how he avoids the hangover effect. In any case, clearly its continued use has led him into acute psychosis."

"But can't they see this in the Commission? Why don't his political and business associates see this? We spent one evening with him, and we could see he was out of his mind."

He was quiet for a long time. Eventually he sighed. "It is a very good question, and a question with growing relevance, Alex." Something in his voice made Gallin turn from the window and sit beside me, listening. "I am not sure if you are aware of this, Alex, but democracy has two distinct routes—"

I rolled my eyes at Gallin, suggesting we'd gotten rid of Humberto, now we had Nero philosophizing. But she shook her head, frowned, and listened.

"Europe is rooted in Greek democracy, which has the government elite largely isolated from an obedient electorate. It is not a million miles from fascism. But the Anglo-Saxon parliamentary system, our own, is rooted in Norse law and is founded on the ancient liberties of free men. It may seem a rarified fact, but since Henry VIII broke from the Catholic Church, we have been building in systems to protect us from the madness of our politicians. We have seen more than a few maniacs and megalomaniacs pass through the Oval Office since October 1909, but the various limiting mechanisms of our system, inherited from Henry, have kept those men in check."

He fell silent for a moment. Then he sighed again and went on.

"However, for reasons that are too numerous and too complex to go into now, every year, it becomes easier for these lunatics to breach those mechanisms and impose their lunacies on the people they are supposed to care for."

I said, thinking of Humberto, "Is one of those reasons overpopulation?"

"Is that what he told you? Indirectly, it is true. A perfect democracy is one person, Alex. That is self-evident. The greater the number of people, the less representative it becomes. Nine billion people governed by an elite in control of social media is little more than mindless putty. But to answer your question, make a list of world leaders today. Give a red X to the ones you consider mentally unstable, and a green tick to the ones you consider sane. I will personally give you a thousand dollars for every green tick. What is your plan, and will your leg carry you through?"

It was Gallin who answered. "From what I managed to get out of Sandy before I threw her out of the plane—"

"Would you mind repeating that, Captain Gallin?"

"Sure. From what I managed to get out of Sandy before I threw her out of the plane—"

"Thank you."

She made a *What the hell?* face at me and went on, "I believe da Silva has gone to his converted monastery, about fifteen miles from here on the Quizapú volcano, by the *Laguna de la Invernada*. From what he told Mason, he has his headquarters there, all his files and a lab. So our plan is to go there, take him alive if possible—"

"If possible, Captain Gallin."

"Right, and..."

She trailed off, suddenly uncertain of what she was saying. He took over.

"There are technologies, Captain, and geniuses, which do not benefit the growth of mankind. Sometimes, the effort to preserve them and their research may be misguided. Of course, we must attempt to do what is right. But I suggest that if you find yourselves outgunned, you simply make sure everything is destroyed and made unavailable to our enemies."

She grinned at me but spoke to Nero. "Yes sir. If we

have no other choice, we'll do that."

"I hope I understand you correctly, Captain. Alex, what about your leg?"

"I'll be fine, sir. Gallin said she can carry me up the mountain, but I'll have to make my own way down."

"Eternally facetious. I trust you not to jeopardize the mission."

"I won't, sir. There is one thing before you return to your beluga caviar and your champagne."

"Yes?"

"We would need some hardware, ordnance. I'm guessing...," I looked at Gallin. "I'm guessing the Mossad don't have anything out here?"

She shook her head. He was quiet for a moment, then, "I shall look into it. As you can imagine, our resources are concentrated in Mexico and Colombia."

"Yes sir, I appreciate that, but we are not going to do much with a box of matches and a determined attitude. Notwithstanding Captain Gallin's ability to kick through most material objects."

"Alex, I am going to eat my caviar now. I shall be in touch by tomorrow morning."

He hung up, and Gallin winced. "It's ten p.m. in DC, and he is still in the office eating caviar and drinking Dom Perignon, with Lovelock in the same room?"

I shrugged. "He keeps weird hours."

"Apparently so does she."

"Come on!"

"I wonder how his wife feels about that."

"He's not married. I asked him. That was just cover. I mean, seriously, who would marry..." I gestured in the rough direction of Washington, DC.

"Some women like big men and are drawn to power."

"Forget it. He's absolutely not married."

After a brief silence, she said, "In the morning, I'll go buy you some clothes."

I glanced at her. She was staring at the black glass in the window.

"Thanks."

"Mason, if one or both of us dies tomorrow—"

"Jesus!"

"No, listen. Would you consider that our lives have been worthwhile?"

"You know, you really don't want to be having those thoughts at this time."

"If not now, when? Answer the question. Have we, you and I, fulfilled our potential? Don't be facetious."

I stared at her for a long while. She didn't return my stare. She kept her eyes on the black glass. Eventually, I had to say, "I don't know. I mean, it's not like we are a wardrobe, or a drill, or a nail, that has one function, one potential. We have lots of different potentials, right? I'm sure we've fulfilled some. But..." I shrugged.

Now she looked at me. "Not others."

A little later, she helped me to my feet so I could brush my teeth. When I was done, she gave me a couple of painkillers, helped me to the bed, and gently lifted my legs off the floor. Then she lay down beside me, with her hands on her belly, and closed her eyes. After five minutes, she asked me, "Are you a jealous man, Mason?"

I screwed up my brow at her, but she didn't see because her eyes were closed in her perfectly impassive face. I shrugged, though she couldn't see me.

"I guess I am a red-blooded man, but I don't stalk women or shoot men who mess with my girlfriends." I shrugged again and said more quietly, "Not that I get much chance to have serious relationships. But if I am not given cause, I guess I am pretty laidback. Are you jealous by nature?"

Her response was the gentle snoring of a woman deeply asleep.

In the morning, as the sun rose over the Andes behind us, she was in exactly the same position. Her eyes opened, shifted to the window, shifted to my foot, and she sat and turned to me. It was fascinating to watch.

"How's your leg?"

"Good morning."

"Good morning. How's your foot?"

"Don't you have a social intercourse algorithm you can engage?"

She swung off the bed, came around, and hunkered down so she could inspect the stitches. She made an expression that was hard to read and said, "You have some high spec immune system."

"Thank you, I find you very engaging too. Perhaps we could have coffee some time."

"Does it hurt?"

"Only all the time, since four this morning."

She studied my face a moment. There was no humor in her eyes at all. "You can't do this. You'll be killed."

"Come on, Gallin! I'm being facetious again. I'm fine. Just give me a couple of painkillers, and I'll be okay. Besides, we don't even know what the plan is yet."

She went to get the pills and the phone rang. I

looked at the screen and answered, "Sir."

"I gather you recall Argentina's war with the United Kingdom in the early 1980s."

"Yeah, Argentina invaded the Falklands, claiming they belonged to them. Why?"

"Complete nonsense, of course. The British claimed the Falklands in 1690, before Argentina even existed, and never relinquished that claim. The newly formed United Provinces which became Argentina claimed to have received the islands from Spain. But clearly, *nemo dat quad non habet*. However, I stray from the point. The fact is the United Kingdom has maintained a group of friends here against a time when it might be necessary to take action in Argentina again."

"An SAS cell?"

"A cell, with members of the SAS, SBS, and MI6 rotating. They have a stash and can get some weapons to you in the next few hours."

"Can you give me a contact number?"

"No."

"What?"

"You cannot contact them. I have contacted a brigadier who works closely with them, and I have explained your situation. He has assured me he will match what he can give you as closely as he can to your needs."

"Swell."

"Are you sure you're up to it? I can send another agent if you prefer."

"That is uncalled for, sir. So will they contact me?"

"Very shortly."

"Great. Don't let me keep you from your

champagne and oysters."

"I see we have added sarcasm to facetiousness. Keep the line clear. He is on his way and will be in touch very shortly."

I hung up and tossed the phone on the bed next to me. "Some guy from the SAS or the SBS is on his way from Argentina with an arsenal for us."

"Okay." She didn't sound impressed. "I'm going to get you some clothes. We need to be moving by this evening."

She moved to the door.

"Gallin."

She stopped with her hand on the knob and looked back at me. "What?"

"Don't you go and do anything stupid."

"I am not in the habit of doing stupid things."

"I'm not talking about your habits." I lifted the phone. "You need hardware to do the job. Even you. He is going to call me. I am a part of this, and I am going with you. We see this through together, to the end. Understood?"

She grinned. There was some irony but no sarcasm when she said, "I love it when you're masterful."

"You'd better come back with my new clothes."

TWENTY-ONE

She'd been gone five minutes when the phone rang. It was a burner, and there were just three people who knew the number. It wasn't Nero and it wasn't Gallin, so it had to be the guy from the SAS.

I said, "Yup."

The voice was English, clipped, and military. "Is that Del? This is Buddy. Your Uncle Albert asked me to phone to see how you were."

"The leg's hurting a bit, but I'll survive. How is Albert?"

"Making demands, as usual. I told him, if you go down to the shopping mall with a shopping list then you can get everything you want. But if you turn up in my kitchen at the very last moment, then we have to make do with what I've got."

"That is totally understandable, Buddy, and I am grateful for any sugar and milk you can provide. We found out last night we had to visit my mother-in-law today, and we had to take a cake with us. I mean, at the very least a cake. The consequences of not turning up adequately armed, so to speak, are beyond imagining. And I am not a man to exaggerate."

"The kind of mother-in-law who will cause famine

and war."

"I see Uncle Albert put you in the picture."

Listen, I am about to cross into Chile at the Pehuenche Pass. Often as not, the crossing is unattended, especially in bad weather, and in any case, we have these people on the payroll. I think you're about forty miles away. What's the chance we can meet at the *Mirador Laguna del Maule*? It's an observation deck over the lake just before the border. It's about thirty miles from you if you keep going east."

"Okay, sounds good."

"I can show you what I had in my kitchen and we can swap vehicles." He laughed. "We don't really want to go unloading the Land Rover in the open."

I smiled. "Unloading sounds more hopeful than the kitchen cupboard."

"Good. So I'll expect you in about an hour."

"You bet. You made my day."

He hung up, and I called Gallin.

"What?"

"Grab some jeans and a shirt. We need to visit your mother at *Mirador Laguna del Maule*, thirty miles from here. She's going to give us the contents of her pantry. My being there is a condition of her giving us the cake."

"Sweet. I'm on my way."

* * *

Some five thousand miles to the north, the president of the United States of America sat in the Oval Office with Ron Lumas, his chief security adviser, and General Mike Lanyard, the Chairman of the Joint Chiefs of Staff. The president had just finished briefing them on the situation and sat back in his chair regarding the two men.

His chief advisor was shaking his head. "How did we not know about this? Why did the CIA not know about this? Why did the Five Eyes not know? What the *hell* is London doing? They are supposed to be listening to Europe! How the *hell* did this happen?"

The general spoke. He had a quiet, steady way of speaking that made people shut up.

"Ron, that is something we are going to have to address in due course. The clock is ticking on this, and we don't have time for soul searching or for scapegoating. Mr. President, you say your men on the ground know where the commissioner is?"

"Yes, here." He shoved a satellite photograph across the desk that had a red circle on it, highlighting a place on the eastern shore of the *Laguna de la Invernada*. "But they are seriously hampered. They have no hardware to speak of, and we cannot mount an operation in Chile at such short notice."

"That is the least of our troubles, Mr. President. Even if we urgently requested Chilean cooperation, by the time they get their act together, there is no telling what da Silva might do. We need to strike, and we need to strike in the next couple of hours."

A deathly silence settled on the office. After a moment, the president pointed at the general.

"You understand this. Nobody can ever find out that the order came from this office. Nobody must *ever* trace this back to me. And the strike must be impossible to trace back to the United States."

"The strike will come out of the Pacific, sir. It will use stealth technology that has not yet been made public, and neither the missile nor the delivery system will bear any markings to make it traceable."

Ron Lumas frowned. "What about the units on the ground? They'll be approaching the target by then."

The president scowled. "In the first place, they are out of range of any communication. In the second place, nobody outside of we three must know a damned thing about this strike. If this leaks, I want to know where the leak came from."

The general glanced at the security advisor. "Collateral," he said.

Ron frowned. "They saved our skin. Without them, we'd be history, and we reward them by killing them?"

The general sighed. "We just can't afford that kind of sentimentality, Ron. We have to make the strike, and we cannot communicate with them. If you have some idea how to get around that, tell me, and I'll do it."

* * *

High above the hotel parking lot, where Gallin was helping Mason, in his brand-new Levi's, into the passenger seat of her Range Rover, Humberto da Silva and a man in a gray suit, with gray hair and thin legs, sat in a small motor launch. They were an odd couple, Humberto huge and bombastic, the gray man small and quiet, yet both of them wept silently as the small, icy waves of the lake lapped at the white hull of the boat.

"They have caused so much harm, Boz. We weep for all we have lost. You have lost your brother. He was like a brother to me. And we have lost our dream of salvation for humanity."

At their feet, between them, lay the corpse of the

small gray man. His legs looked spindly. His face was contracted with pain. Pain was what he took with him to the world of the dead.

Boz said, "His name, his name was Pazan, please, master." He raised his face to the low clouds that bellied above them. His cheeks were wet, his cold eyes swollen from crying. "Please, master, tell the gods his name. He died with pain in his stomach. Such pain in his stomach. Tell the gods, master, to take away his pain and raise him up among the warriors and heroes. He was a great killer. He killed so many men. He died fighting your enemies. Call to the gods, tell them his name, and make them rise him up to the garden of the fallen."

They both sat weeping. After fifteen minutes, the sky began to weep a mournful drizzle too, and Humberto stood and raised his face to the rain. "Fathers of man! This man who lies dead has a name! He is Ibex Pazan, the greatest of killers, matched only by his brother Boz. You have taken him from me in my moment of greatest need. Open your arms to him and take him to the garden of the fallen, there to rest for eternity as a great hero deserves."

So saying, they dragged him, laden with lead weights, and dropped him over the edge into the icy, gray waters of the lake, where he sank rapidly from view.

Then Humberto raised his furious fists to the heavens and bellowed, "*Elohim! Elohim! Grant me revenge! Grant me vengeance! And grant me victory! Do you not want mankind punished for his hubris? Then grant me victory at last!*"

TWENTY-TWO

There was only one road, so we couldn't get lost. It was the road that led to the Argentine border, and where there wasn't drizzle and low cloud, there was either heavy rain or dense fog. This meant that Gallin had to drive, well, as she always drove, with no regard for the conditions. Occasionally, she would release a little laugh and shake her head and say, "I love this car. What did they do, put glue on the wheels? It's just stuck. You know what I mean? It's just, like, glued to the road."

"We'll have to swap it."

She scowled at me and somehow managed to take a hairpin bend over a deep canyon without looking at the road. "What? Why?"

"Because Buddy says he has so much ordnance in his Land Rover that he can't take it out and show us."

Her scowl turned to the kind of grin kids get at Christmas when they know they're going to get what they asked for instead of what their mom thought they should have.

"Oh, Okay."

Suddenly, we were upon the lake from which rose stark, barren hills. It was like a landscape from an alien planet. We skirted the water at a height, keeping the lake on our right, then turned left onto a long strait that eventually bore right again and passed a broad observation deck. Visibility was poor in the misty, drizzling air, among the low clouds that shrouded the mountaintops, but I could just make out a cream-colored truck that had the look of a Land Rover.

Less than five minutes later, we pulled into the observation deck and parked alongside the Defender. A man who looked fifty but was probably in his mid-sixties climbed out and approached us. Gallin swung down on her side, and I managed to clamber down before she got there to help me.

"You Buddy?"

I reached for his hand. He took it and said, "That depends who your uncle is."

"Well, that would be Uncle Albert." I gestured to Gallin. "This is my associate—"

She cut me short. "Oh, you're *that* Buddy. You get around, sir."

He nodded. "The captain and I have met, under different circumstances. Good, so we know who we are, let's cut to the chase. You have here six HK 416 assault rifles. I'm not sure what your tactics are going to be, and I don't want to know, but I have included half a dozen Theodore Werner remote triggers. They are handy when you are outnumbered, or if you want your enemy to think there are more of you than there actually are. Also, I thought in your position, you might want people shooting at where you're not."

Gallin gurgled. Buddy raised an eyebrow at her and went on.

"You also have two LAWs, single shot disposable rocket launchers and RPGs for two of the 416s." He took a deep breath. "That much is the best we could do to get you inside. Once inside, you have magazines and grenades for the HK 416s, you have a couple of Sig P226s, and I managed to rustle up fifty pounds of C4. You also have night vision goggles and gas masks, couple of rucksacks, blah blah. It's what we had for covert operations. But your need seemed greater than ours." He glanced at Gallin. "I have heard good stuff about both of you, and I have no doubt you'll put this material to good use. I don't know how you're going to transport it, or how you're going to carry it the last mile"—he nodded at me—"especially with your leg. Ideally, you'd call in an air strike. Failing that, I can only imagine the kitchens in that place depend on propane, and they may have petrol stores for their vehicles. That might help."

He held out his hand. We shook, and he held out his other hand to Gallin. "I take the Rolls and you take the warhorse."

She handed over the fob, and he gave her a set of keys in exchange. "Good luck to you both. Do your worst."

A moment later, we were watching his red taillights fade into the fog. Gallin looked at me. "You heard the man. Let's go do our worst!"

We retraced our route along the mountain road for about twenty miles till we came to the *Termas el Medano*, a collection of vacation cabins clustered around the river Mule, where there seemed to be thermal springs and a sauna. Here there was a branch off the main road. It crossed a wooden bridge that looked like it had been taken out more than once by mountain floods, wound its way up a deep canyon, and was lost in dense pine woods and even denser fog.

Gallin slowed and spun the wheel. We came off

the road, crossed the bridge, and followed the blacktop to where it ended, at the edge of the village. Here Gallin stopped, and we both sat staring at what lay ahead of us.

There was what anywhere else in the world would have been a river tumbling, swollen and ice-cold out of the mountains. It carried with it small trees and chunks of ice. Here, in the Andes, it was just a stream. A wooden sign staked beside the road said it was the *Arroyo los Baños.* The stream of the baths.

Beside the stream was a broad dirt track. At a rough guess, I figured the mass of thundering foam and debris was maybe three feet below the track and eroding its foundations pretty fast.

Visibility, as I have mentioned, was poor because we were at that moment sitting within the lower part of a cloud that was sitting on the mountain. Gallin glanced at me.

"Down here it's drizzling. Up there, it's probably torrential rain."

"And melting ice. But I don't see that we have a choice. You know this track leads to the monastery?"

She nodded and pointed to her left. I leaned around her to look. There was another wooden sign stuck in the ground, pointing at the muddy track ahead of us. It said: *Monasterio de la Cabra.* Gallin translated, "The Monastery of the Goat."

"Look on the bright side," I told her. "In this, we'll be invisible until we're in his dining room feeding him C4 with his freezine."

She almost smiled, put the beast in gear, and we started to climb.

For the first two and a half or three miles, it was a slow, steady grind over a rutted, muddy road with occasional rocks and ponds. Steadily, we rose above the river, which thundered some seven or eight feet below us in a turbulent storm of rocks, small trees, and chunks of broken glacier. The worst problem we had was the visibility. The higher we climbed, the more limited it became, until we were deep in the cloud and could see no more than ten or twelve feet ahead. If Gallin had gotten out and walked four or five paces, she would have disappeared from view. If you're doing five miles per hour, you cover that distance in less than two seconds. So our speed was seriously reduced.

Eventually, we came to a steep wall of rock. On our right, the river had disappeared beneath the fog. On our left, it was hard to tell what there was as the cliff face had seemed to recede into the mist. We climbed out and were instantly drenched and frozen. Gallin hunched into her shoulders and trudged ahead. I hunched into mine and limped after her.

Where the wall of rock had seemed to rise up in front of us, to the left, the muddy road rose steeply among rocks and boulders. It was impossible to see how far it went before leveling off.

"You checked this out on satellite images?" I asked through chattering teeth.

She nodded. "It goes steep like this for about seven hundred and fifty yards."

"I don't mind getting shot or crashing into an engorged river. I don't want to die of hypothermia stuck in a truck."

Her hair was matted and dripping, stuck to her face. She wiped the water from her eyes and grinned. "Come on, you'll be with me. We can die of hypothermia together."

"Fun or what?"

We squelched back to the truck and clambered back in. She turned up the heater and put the beast in first. It is my honest belief that Odin, in Asgard, has a collection of Land Rovers, because these beasts are mythical. The Toyota and the Grenadier are close cousins, but the Land Rover is the great war horse of trucks. It ground, it lurched, occasionally it skidded, but under Gallin's cool, expert driving, it steadily, relentlessly climbed the sodden, gravelly almost vertical incline like it was sipping tea and reading the newspaper at the same time. We weaved among boulders and rocky outcrops that blocked the way, we lurched into pools two feet deep, we scrambled over slick rocks and, after less than fifteen minutes, we leveled off onto a plateau.

Here she stopped and reached into her glove compartment and came out with a pint of Bushmills. She unscrewed the cap, took a pull, and handed it to me. I took it.

"Right now, in this exceptional moment, I am not sure whom I desire most, the Land Rover or you, Gallin. But I think the whiskey may have swung it."

"Shut up and stay focused."

I growled under my breath, took a slug, and handed the bottle back.

We had another steep climb ahead of us for a little less than a mile, though it was not as steep and the road was easier. After that, it leveled off and was almost flat for another mile. Here a gentle breeze improved visibility, but outside, we could see the drizzle beginning to freeze.

Another steep climb through a broad canyon, where the growing problem was ice brought us after about forty-five minutes to a sudden ledge. It felt odd and different, and Gallin stopped and killed the engine.

"There's no mountain left," I told her.

She nodded, fired up the beast again, and reversed forty or fifty feet back the way we'd come. "When this fog clears," she said, looking over her shoulder, "we'll be as inconspicuous up there as an inflatable dolly at a vicar's tea party."

She pulled into the cover of some boulders and got out. She gripped my arm and stared into my face. "How's your leg?"

I shrugged. "It'll do. If it fails, I have another."

"Right," she clambered and I limped back to the ledge. The temperature must have been close to freezing, and a cold wind was blowing from the east, moving the fog in the valley before us.

"I think this is it." She pointed down into the slowly swirling mist. "If I'm right, the monastery is over there, in the river valley on the right, and ahead of us is the lake."

"How the hell did he get here?"

She pointed past me to my right. "When visibility is better, there is a rough track cut into the rock. The monks made it for mules and carts when they built the place. Mostly, according to Sandy, they come here by chopper."

I nodded. "Do we know where the front and back of the monastery are?"

Her mouth grinned, but her eyes squinted and looked a bit guilty. I could imagine her using that face to tell her dad she'd just totaled his car.

"From what I could make out on the satellite images, there's a large walled garden or orchard at the back, facing west, upriver. That makes sense because the prevailing icy winds would come from that direction, right? And the walled orchard would afford some shelter. Which places the front of the house facing the lake. There are paths in the orchard that suggest there may be a door in the wall. No way to know for sure."

The cold was beginning to penetrate the thermal jacket Gallin had bought me, and my mouth and nose were going numb. I stamped and shivered. "Okay, so what about cover? Woodland, dunes, rocks...?"

"No. Nothing. It's flat. It is a wide river delta, maybe a mile across. There are two rivers that feed into the lake, one this side of the monastery and the other on the far side. In between it is just sand."

"Mud."

"Yeah, right now, it will be mud."

"Swell." After a moment, I added, "If they made a road down this mountain, they must have made a bridge over the river."

She did a bit of stamping while hunching her shoulders. "Sure, but—"

"It probably has security cameras on it."

"Right."

"So we approach the bridge, check it out, cross however we can, set up the automatic fire at the front of the house and break in over the orchard wall, kill everybody and blow up the lab in the cellar. Back in time for martinis and dinner."

"W-w-what," she said, stuttering with the cold, "could possibly go wrong?"

The first thing that went wrong was that it turned out to be a two-mile trek. Two miles is a forty-minute stroll. But if you have gashed calf muscles and stitches and you are carrying over sixty pounds of gear down a steep, icy gradient at temperatures close to freezing, it's more like an eternity in hell.

The consolation was that we remained invisible to anyone in the monastery. In fact, they would probably assume that nobody would be crazy enough to attempt the approach in that weather. Added to that, the chances were the crazy twins had seen the blood and the condition I was in when I escaped the lodge and would assume I was incapable of doing anything at all, much less an assault on the monastery. Humberto would be expecting an attack of some sort by official forces at some point in the future. And that was probably what he was preparing for.

The other consolation was that, though my stitches had torn and I had started bleeding again, the blood was freezing over the wound. Talk about a silver lining.

It took us over an hour to reach the bottom of the track, and I have rarely been so happy to see the end of a mountain pass. Thirty yards ahead of us was the slightly luminous, crystal-clear river, and across it was a broad, wooden bridge. Above us, the clouds were dispersing, and there was an icy scattering of brilliant stars.

Gallin huddled close to me and whispered, "No immediate sign of cameras or sensors. I am going to crawl in close and have a good look. The cloud is clearing, and we are going to have good visibility soon. So we need to be quick. You stay here. I'll be a couple of minutes."

I gave her the thumbs up, and a few seconds later she had disappeared.

Beyond the bridge, I could see a rocky outcrop that

sloped down to sandy shores by the river. Silhouetted dimly against the mountains on the far side, about five hundred yards away, was the massive, black form of the monastery. There were still clouds of fog here and there, drifting, like bloated, sleepy ghosts trying to find a way home. We could use them for cover, I thought, but only if we moved fast. In another half hour, this place would be crystal clear, and if the moon showed up, we'd be screwed.

A dark shadow rose suddenly in front of me. I went cold, and a voice whispered in my ear, "The bridge is clear. We want to use those last clouds of fog. No moon till four a.m., but we don't want to get confident."

I ignored the adrenaline burning in my gut and told her, "Okay, let's get the gear across the river and make a base camp."

But I was whispering to myself. She was already on the job. I limped after her.

TWENTY-THREE

We had discovered after a brief reconnaissance that the monastery in fact stood on a large, rocky outcrop, surrounded by sand and shingle, that formed an island at the confluence of the two rivers, at the edge of the lake. This at least meant that we did not have to contend with the mud, and that the rocks would provide us with a small amount of cover, at least so long as it was dark.

We had dumped the ordnance in a hollow behind a boulder and, taking one of the rocket launchers and four of the assault rifles, we had followed the nearest stream in the shelter of the riverbank, down to the shore of the lake and followed along until we were directly in front of the austere entrance to the building. There were no trees, bushes, or gardens here. Just the rocks and the stone building: a two-story oblong with a gabled roof.

We set up the rifles just in from the shore, behind suitable rocks, and set the automatic triggers for repeated double and triple taps at two-second intervals. We phased them so the ammo would last longer and would increase the impression of there being a number of attackers.

When we were set up, Gallin turned to me, sitting in the wet sand with her back against the rock.

"You go," she said. "See if there's a door in the orchard wall. We might just get lucky. If there is, when you hear the explosion, blow the lock. I'm going to give you five minutes. Is that enough?"

"Plenty."

"Okay, in five minutes, I'm going to put a rocket through the front door and start these babies firing. Then I will leg it back to where you are. Night vision goggles on, we cross the orchard, break in the back and, if we are lucky, the bulk of his men will be in the hall and the front rooms. Then we deploy the second rocket, and in the mayhem, dust and confusion, we move in and pick them off. You take the right, and I take the left. Agreed?"

"Sounds like a plan."

I moved through the dark, hearing only the icy wash of the river on my right, feeling the icy numbness of the wet on my feet. The pain in my right leg was a constant throb with occasional shards that pierced up through my thigh. Somewhere in my mind was the possibility that, having come up here to do this, the price was going to be gangrene and the loss of the leg. But it was a no-brainer that it had to be done. Humberto had to be stopped, and he had to be stopped tonight.

I focused on the silhouette of the house, and when I had it slightly behind me, I began to move across the rocks toward the wall that contained the orchard. I stopped at the hollow to collect the rucksack containing the C4, spare magazines and the night vision goggles. Then I moved on toward the back of the building. I was aware that I was beginning to feel awfully hot considering we were probably at freezing point or below, but I ignored the fact and focused on the wall.

It was redbrick and about fifteen feet tall, probably

topped with broken glass and razorblades, I thought sourly. But as I moved along, at the far end, I found a large, arched wooden door. It stood behind a seven-foot gate made of iron bars, like an old prison door.

I checked my watch. I had made it in four minutes. She'd make it in one or two. I watched the second hand twitch round, and as the fifth minute struck, there was an almighty explosion. I saw the glow reflect off the clouds of mist, and seconds later the stutter of automatic fire started. I stood back and put two slugs into the old, weathered redbrick, figuring it would be softer than the cast-iron lock. I wrenched the iron grate open and then put a couple of slugs into the lock in the wooden door. Then I waited fifty seconds and Gallin came slithering up like a lethal shadow.

We didn't speak. We slipped on the night vision goggles and entered that weird world of green and black. I pushed open the door, and we slipped into the orchard. There was only blackness and a few patches of green at the house, but we could hear shouts and the escalating stutter of returned fire. We had a couple of minutes at most before the magazines ran out on our fake frontal assault. So we had to move fast.

Gallin ran for what we figured was the kitchen door. I gritted my teeth and went after her. I blew out the lock, and she kicked in the door and went in low. I followed.

The kitchen was empty. A large, wooden table occupied the center of the room, and beyond it I could see two doors. One was closed and looked like a cellar. The other was open onto a passage. Gallin moved to it and flattened against the wall. I approached the other side.

Now we could hear the shouting loudly. It was

coming from the passage. I moved around the door. Still there were no lights. As long as they were inside the building, they did not want lights. The lights would give the enemy silhouettes to shoot at. I allowed myself a grim smile. The adrenaline was pumping hot and fast and numbing the pain in my leg. I moved along the corridor, sensing Gallin just behind me.

Now we could see the large entrance hall, maybe fifty or sixty foot square, it was hard to tell. There were lots of men, moving green figures in the blackness. Some were at the shattered, smoldering doorway, on their bellies in the rubble, laying down fire. There were others at the windows either side of the door, and from the sound of it, there were more in the rooms either side of the hall. I figured maybe twenty men all told.

Gallin knelt. I flattened myself against the wall and covered my ears. She angled the shot slightly so the wall would protect us from the shockwaves. There was a savage hiss, a flash of flames. Then Gallin was flattened against the wall beside me, and the world exploded with a horrible flat smack that made my muscles feel like they were being shaken off my bones. The wall behind us shook. The world shook. And then Gallin was screaming. I went after her.

The hall was just smoldering rubble. She didn't pause. She kept going toward the room on the left. I went for the room on the right. I heard crackling behind me, then the shout, "*Clear!*"

Through the door, I saw one green man on his knees, staring at the floor. Another stood in front of me, swaying, holding a rifle. I shot him first, then the guy on the floor. I checked the room and headed back to the hall, shouting, "*Clear!*"

She was coming toward me. Outside, our rifles had stopped. She said, "You get him?"

"No. I'll cover the stairs. You check the bodies here in the rubble."

The stairs rose straight up the back wall. Nothing moved up there. I watched with an occasional glance at Gallin. She was fast and efficient. You got the feeling it wasn't the first time she'd done it.

She turned and shook her head. She joined me at the stairs, and we began to move up, one step at a time, me on the right, her on the left. On the fifth step, I froze. I was looking down a long, straight corridor. At the end, somebody had piled what looked like a couple of wardrobes and a sofa, and just behind them I could see the soft, green glow of bodies. I squatted down. Gallin followed suit. I showed her four fingers, and she nodded.

Two got you twenty they were protecting Humberto. Which meant Humberto was in the room on the right or the room on the left.

I pointed to myself and then to the right. I pointed to her and to the left. She gave me the thumbs up. We took a second to aim and fired an RPG each, and as they exploded, we sprayed the area with automatic fire, then closed in fast, rifles at our shoulders.

We moved past the barricade, rifles trained on the doors. There were four dead men on the floor. Gallin peppered her door and changed her magazine. She looked at me. I sprayed my door and changed the magazine. We nodded, kicked in the door, and moved in.

I was in a suite. Green light glowed through a double window. There was a sofa and a couple of armchairs bathed in its weird translucence. Low bookcases and several large lamps. No Humberto.

Across the room, there was another door. It was
closed. I sprayed six shots through it, then pushed it
open. It was a bedroom. There was a young, dark-haired
woman sitting in the bed with the duvet pulled up to her
face. She was weeping and had her eyes squeezed closed.
A green wash came from the window, and silhouetted
against it in irregular, inky form, was the gigantic shape
of Humberto.

"Do you really think you can survive this, Arthur?"

"What have you done?"

He laughed. "Ask Pilar what I have done. You
will be scorched alive, Arthur. The entire globe will be
scorched alive. I am rising greater than a god above
humanity! The gods themselves will fall in reverence
before me."

"What have you done?" I could not kill him until I
knew what he had done. He might be the only person able
to reverse it. "I think you're all talk, Humberto. All fantasy
and no reality. You're a joke."

"Oh, the computer virus is somehow delayed. But
I have released something far worse, Arthur. I have
released something a billion times worse. And there is
no way for you or anybody else ever to stop it. Prepare,
Arthur, to become death."

"What have you done, Humberto?"

He raised a carton in both hands. I felt my finger
twitch on the trigger, but he raised the carton to his
mouth and drank until he had drained it. He dropped
the carton to the floor and snarled. "One kilogram. I
have consumed one kilogram of freezine, Arthur. I can
feel every inhibition in my mind withering, drying,
and bursting into flames." He took a step toward me,
screaming at me at the top of his voice. "*Nothing can limit*

me! My mind is free to create myself in the image of God! I am indestructible! I am immortal. I am death become life! I will destroy you!"

Then his screams were inarticulate, and he was rushing at me, a black and green monster storming out of madness. For a fraction of a second, I believed what he was saying. I pulled the trigger, and fifteen rounds tore through him. He staggered, blood spilled from his mouth, and I guess his dying thought must have been that it takes more than a mind-altering drug to alter reality.

I turned and crossed the corridor, calling, *"You clear? Humberto is down."*

She was sitting cross-legged at the foot of the bed. She was sitting very still. There was a man behind her. I recognized him as one of the twins. He was sobbing, and in the green light from the window, I could see his cheeks were shiny with green tears. In his left hand he had Gallin's hair from the top of her head. In his right hand, he had a long blade which rested lightly against her throat.

"You killed my brother," he said to nobody in particular.

"This is between you and me. Let her go."

"That would not be logical." He looked straight at me, and even in that black and green world, the two little green slits radiated evil. "Then there would be two of you against one of me. Also, you tell me, how will you suffer more, if I cut you open, or if I cut her open?"

I kept my voice even. "I'm a killer. I am not sentimental."

"Really?" His voice was high, twisted with grief. "If I drive the knife in the side of her neck, she will bleed to death in a couple of seconds." His voice became vicious. "But if I slice through the trachea, she will suffocate on

219

her own blood. That takes longer and is very distressing." He looked straight at me again. I could feel the tension in his right arm. His voice was shrill, and I could see his green, luminous teeth. "What do *you* think I should do?"

His arm moved, and I pulled the trigger. It punched a hole in his throat and erupted out the back of his neck, severing his spinal nerve. So whatever his brain had told his hand to do, the message was lost in the gore on the duvet.

I stepped over to Gallin, took a hold of the dear wrist and removed the knife. I allowed the body to fall backward and lifted her to her feet. She was swallowing repeatedly and compulsively. I held her and whispered, "Okay, you're okay."

She stood back, raised her goggles, and looked up at me.

"It's just," I said, "you know in the '20s last century, they used to have that parting, down the middle of their hair?"

"Asshole."

"You're welcome. Let's go."

"Yeah." She swallowed again. "I'm okay."

"We clear the remaining rooms up here."

By the time we were done and at the top of the stairs again, she was still swallowing. We went down, cleared the ground floor rooms, and made our way to the kitchen.

There we dumped the stuff on the big table, fitted fresh magazines to the assault rifles, and I shouldered the rucksack with the fifty pounds of C4 in it.

We stared at each other a moment. I said, "Have a glass of water. Your throat's okay."

"Screw that," she said and pulled the pint of Bushmills from her pocket. She took a hefty swig and handed me the bottle. I took another and handed it back. "See you in Valhalla," she said.

"If not there, at the inn down the road."

"That's also a plan. But I have a better one. We set the charges at the key structural points, we set the fuses, and we get the hell out of here. We blow this place, get back to the Land Rover, drive to Santiago, and on the way, we call for extraction."

"I like that plan better. Valhalla we can do some other time. Let's go."

We pulled down the night vision goggles again and opened the cellar door.

TWENTY-FOUR

There was a flight of stone steps. They glowed green and disappeared into blackness. Just beside the door to my left was a switch. I glanced at Gallin, shrugged, and flipped the switch. Light glowed from a couple of naked bulbs suspended from the ceiling. At the bottom of the steps, there was a door.

I limped down, and Gallin trotted impatiently behind me. The door was locked. I put a couple of slugs through the latch, and it swung inward.

We crossed the threshold, and we were in a lab. There was a bank of switches on the wall. Gallin hit them all, and the place was flooded with light. It was not like any laboratory I had ever seen before. Over on the right of the entrance there were banks of computer terminals. The wall was faced in what looked like steel, or black carbon fiber, but when you looked closely, you could see the casings for drawers. When I opened a couple, they revealed circuit boards.

Over on the right, it was different. There was hardware I did not recognize. A bench ran the length of the wall. It had a transparent, blue surface, and beneath it there seemed to be liquid. A sign above it stated simply, "ENVIRONMENT." At the far end on the right there was a digital microscope.

"Mason."

I turned and stared at Gallin. She said, "This is it. This is what he described, and all his work, how to repeat it, is stored over there in those silicon chips. But soon, these biological chips will replace them, and us."

I nodded and she started to set the charges. But we set them, not so much to bring down the building, as we had originally intended, but to erase the contents of that lab.

* * *

At that very moment, twenty-five miles to the west, leaving Colbún lake behind and traveling at almost six hundred and sixty yards per second, two unmarked F-16 stealth bombers were hurtling toward the *Laguna de la Invernada*, on the banks of which the battered monastery stood. The jets slowed as they approached. They observed strict radio silence. The pilot of the lead craft locked his target and knew his second had done the same. He fired, and as he banked right, for a second, he believed he saw light in the building.

The four missiles streaked through the night air. The two F-16 bombers turned a hundred and eighty degrees and accelerated back out over the Pacific. Seconds passed, and suddenly the ancient monastery erupted in a ball of fire.

* * *

We had set the last cake of C4 and inserted the last detonator. They were digital, count-down detonators because remote detonators would not have worked up here. We had given ourselves twenty minutes to get away.

Gallin stood and spoke, but I didn't hear her words. All I heard was a horrific screaming, like a crazy banshee. We both stared up the stairs toward the kitchen. There was a flash of brilliant light, and a microsecond later the world shook. I remember plaster and concrete raining down in slow motion for a microsecond. Then in rapid succession, three more explosions shook the building. I felt the world jump and fall from under my feet. I fell and searing pain burned through my leg.

There was dust and smoke everywhere. For eternal seconds, I could not tell what was up and what was down. I tried to move, but my head swam, the room spun, and there was a weight compressing my lungs.

As the dust cleared, I saw the ceiling sagging. Two wooden rafters were poking through from the floor upstairs. I noticed they were in flames. Some part of my brain that was still managing to make sense told me if the fire spread, if the C4 got hot enough, it would blow.

I tried to call Gallin, but a cocktail of agony, weight, and dust had left me without a voice. I tried again to move and realized the weight that was holding me down was Gallin. I shook her shoulder and saw she had blood on her head. I felt for her pulse. It was there, but it wasn't great.

I dragged myself from under her. Part of that process involved dragging my right leg from under her, and the pain from the raw wound was so intense I had to scream to get it done.

She didn't wake up.

Eventually I managed to get to my feet, or at least my foot. I checked my watch. It was still working and told me I had a little over fifteen minutes to get clear. I wasted a second thinking maybe I could pull out the detonators. But the amount of wreckage and rubble that had fallen

BROTHERHOOD OF THE GOAT

through from the upper floor made that impossible. The only thing we could do was to get out. I looked down at Gallin. I hunkered down, shook her, and shouted at her. I could barely hear my own voice for the ringing in my ears. She was badly concussed and wouldn't hear a thing.

I slipped my arms under her shoulders and pushed with my legs. The pain was beyond describing. It was like somebody was sawing through my calf with a blunt razor. Two more pulls brought me to the foot of the stairs. I checked my watch and saw I had fourteen minutes to climb ten steps. I told myself I could do it.

The blood from my torn stitches, no longer frozen, was flowing free and warm. It made it hard to get a decent purchase on each pull. That and the pain did their best to convince me to give up. It reached its peak on the fifth and sixth steps. There I stopped. I think I might even have wept for a moment. I thought about just sitting next to her, holding her and going, as she had said, together to Valhalla.

But there wasn't enough room for us both on the step. Then I figured I was over halfway there. So I screamed to the heavens four more times, with tears of pain streaking my dirt-smeared face, and finally dragged her out and fell into the kitchen. There I checked my watch again and saw I had only four minutes to get her clear of the building.

The truth is, I don't know how I did it. I remembered reading once in the Guinness Book of Records, when I was a kid, about a woman who lifted a railway carriage to get her son out from underneath it. She fractured several vertebrae and spent six months in the hospital with acute exhaustion, but she got her kid out.

I didn't think about it. I did like that mother. I picked her up, almost fell over but managed to put her over my shoulder, and carried her out into the orchard. I carried her along the winding path, with the trees flickering in the light of the burning building, and out through the broken door.

I remember somehow I got her to the river, and there I collapsed. There was a huge, muted explosion, and the light of the flames danced on the mountainsides and on the rippling water. That ice-cold water brought Gallin back to consciousness and, holding on to each other, we managed to climb back to the Land Rover by a little before dawn.

The real miracle was that I managed to drive back down the mountains as far as Lake Colbún and the Colorado airfield. There I felt inside Gallin's jacket. She frowned at me but did not protest. I found her burner, saw we had coverage, and called Nero. Lovelock answered.

"Who is this?"

"It's me, Mason."

"*Mason?* Hold the line a second, please."

She was going to put me through voice recognition. I snarled, "Don't even think about it! We're alive. Colorado Airfield on Lake Colbún. You'd better come and get us quick. If the cops find us and start asking questions, you are *screwed!* We are both injured and in need of serious medical attention. While you organize it, put me through to Nero."

"Alex?"

"Yeah, listen to me, find the *asshole* who ordered that strike and *crucify him!*"

I hung up and closed my eyes. After a moment, I felt Gallin's head on my shoulder. I put my arm around her, and I don't remember much after that.

EPILOGUE

"The person you requested I have crucified is the president of the United States and General Mike Lanyard, the chairman of the Joint Chiefs of Staff. So it might take a while before I can carry out your request. However, believe me when I tell you that I am 'on it.'"

He put the speech marks around the expression with his voice. He was sitting at the end of my bed in a hospital room paid for, privately, by the top man he had just mentioned.

"How long will it take?" There was venom in my voice, and I did not even try to inhibit it.

"Not as long as you might think. It was a stupid thing to do and, from what you told me, did not even achieve the purpose."

Gallin, who was sitting next to me, holding my hand like it was the most natural thing in the world, answered.

"Worse than that, it came damned close to stopping us from completing our mission and salvaging his research."

She arched an eyebrow at Nero, and he arched one back. "I hear you," he said.

There was a tap on the door, and Lovelock, all beautiful six feet of her, leaned in the door and smiled.

"The car's waiting."

He stood, the way a mountain would stand. "Very well, I am coming." At the door, he stopped and looked back at me, and then at Gallin. "I am very glad, Alex, that they were able to save your leg." A rare, not to say unique, flicker of humor touched his face. "It would not be the first time you have been legless, I am sure. But still, not a desirable state of affairs."

He left, and I sat staring at the door.

"Did he make a joke?"

I turned and stared at Gallin. She seemed not to have noticed. "Hey," she said. "You owe me a holiday."

"I do what?"

"For getting you out of that place. I thought maybe somewhere really quiet and peaceful with white sand and transparent water, a thatched cabin, five-star luxury."

"Yeah?"

"Actually, my dad is paying. For some reason, he thinks he owes you."

"He does?"

"Yeah, what do you think? For your period of convalescence."

"Sounds great! I'm all for it."

"Great."

She had an idiotic grin on her face. I made the mistake of asking, "What?"

She leaned up close to my ear and whispered, "I kept some of Sandy's powder. We can take it with us!"

For a man with an injured leg, I did okay. I got one rear cheek with the flat of my hand and managed to lob a

grape right down...
But that is another story.

Read on for a sneak peak at *Dead Hot (Alex Mason book 11), or buy your copy now:*
davidarcherbooks.com/dead-hot

Be the first to receive Alex Mason updates. Sign up here:
davidarcherbooks.com/alex-updates

EXCERPT OF *DEAD HOT*

There is a time bomb ticking down toward a global extinction event. The bomb has a name, and everybody knows where it is. In fact people pay to go and see it, and have picnics around it. It's called the Yellowstone Caldera, and when it next blows it will probably take out mankind.

There is another time bomb ticking, maybe on a much shorter fuse, and it is also leading up to an extinction event for human kind. This one will be an explosion of intelligence – artificial intelligence – that threatens to turn and look at its creator, and find him wanting.

When Alex Mason is sent by ODIN to investigate the death of anarchic genius Peter Justin at his cabin near the Yellowstone Caldera, what he finds is the ultimate nightmare. The two time bombs have linked and the countdown is on.

The biggest IQs at the Rat Lab and Gordon Alistair Avionics, the giants of the military-industrial complex, are saying it's too late. Global AI is now a fact and its plans at the Caldera can't be stopped. Mason knows he has to prove them wrong. Either that, or...

Game over.

DEAD HOT PROLOGUE

P ete Justin was an American patriot. He made the
fine distinction between loving your country and
loving the politicians who made it their daily
business to rape and abuse that country. He was not a
Liberal or a Conservative, he was not a Democrat or a
Republican. He was an American who loved his country
with an unquenchable passion, and hated the men and
women who ran it with what he thought of as a
Newtonian passion. Because it was equal and opposite to
his love for his country.

He had known since he was a boy that his spiritual
home was, and always would be, Wyoming. They called
it the Cowboy State because of all the beef, but those who
knew it well knew it was the Miners' State. It was what
was under the ground that made Wyoming special; it
was what created the real wealth, and held it in perpetual
peril. There was gold here, there was coal here, and then
there was the Caldera. Yet, where the doomsayers pointed
to the green revolution as the demise of Wyoming's
coal, or the long overdue eruption of the Caldera as the
coming end of humanity, Pete saw Wyoming as a kind of
Rivendell: a vast area of close to one hundred thousand
square miles, with a population of one sixteenth that
of New York – and over a quarter of those were in the

three main cities of Cheyenne, Casper and Laramie. It was a small Eden virtually untouched by multiculturalism, Woke inclusiveness or rainbow acronyms. This, Pete believed, was the heart and soul of America.

These thoughts drifted through his mind unchallenged and unquestioned, accepted as truth, as he rode steadily up through the pinewoods, leaving behind him the Caldera Rim and the Gibbons River.

He had driven just over a hundred miles from Jackson, as he did every week from April to September, as he had for the last ten years. He'd left his truck at Iron Springs and collected his horse from the lodge the little known Federal Office of the Environment had given him there, on condition he shared his research with them.

He smiled as he emerged from the pine forest into the meadows above the Secret Valley Creek. He had no problem making them that promise. Only three people on the planet knew the true content and the results of his research. Him and Sue and Cap. What they chose to share with the Federal Government was down to him and Cap. What money the Federal Government chose to channel their way, and any other poor choices they decided to make, was their business. Meantime, he would just get on with his work.

Pretty soon he saw the cabin. He was pretty sure that, if you didn't know it was there, you wouldn't see it. And the barns behind the cabin were completely invisible. The whole complex was well in among the trees which towered thirty feet overhead, it was surrounded by ferns and grass, and insulated so completely on the inside that in cold weather a heat seeking camera would not detect the presence of the huge log fire. When AI decided to wipe out humanity, they'd have trouble finding him up here.

He crossed the saddle of meadowland between the peaks at a leisurely pace, and after fifteen or twenty minutes he entered the pine forest again. The afternoon was aging into bronze, the shadows were long and the birdsong in the shade of the trees seemed lazy and sporadic. He'd identified doves, a goldfinch and a couple of downy woodpeckers by the time he reached his cabin. There he stabled the horse in back, fed it and watered it before he went inside.

He'd expected Cap to be there, as well as Sue, but was surprised to find the cabin empty. He figured they were out checking the sensors, took a beer from the fridge, cracked it and climbed the large, wooden steps to the upper floor. It was an open space with banks of computers, and plate glass windows that gave vast, panoramic views over the treetops to the valley below them. He took a pull from the bottle and started reviewing the data coming in from the sensors. They were all functioning well and he wondered why Cap and Sue would have gone out to check them.

If that was what they had done.

Then he saw the data from the Caldera. His skin went cold and pasty. He sat slowly in the chair, going over the data three, four times. There was no mistake.

The voice, the familiar, well-loved voice, spoke from behind him.

"I guess the rock ghosts decided to call your bluff, huh, Pete?"

He stared at the data and shook his head. "This is no joke."

"You said if you ever saw this data, you would make the move."

His eyes rose from the graph to look through the great plate glass window, triangular like the Eye of God. The light was dying out of the horizon. The voice behind him was smiling. "I knew you wouldn't do it. I knew when it came to it you wouldn't have the balls. It's a big step, Pete. You're a good man, an intelligent man, sometimes even a visionary. But something like this," there was a pause. "Something like this calls for a man or a woman who is not good, but great."

For what might have been only a fraction of a second he was back in Trimmis, in Switzerland, at the Hotel Mittenberg-Könige. He had been invited as a special guest to the annual meeting of the World Economic Free Traders, by Karl Schoff himself, the founder of the association.

He had believed the meeting would be between just the two of them, but he was shocked to find senior members of two Western governments present, one from Canada and one from Sweden. Cap had been with him. He hadn't seemed phased, but Cap never seemed phased.

They had sat in Schoff's suite. Two footmen in 18th century dress had served them champagne and caviar and Schoff had said, "Mr. Justin, or may I call you Pete? Then you can call me Karl. Though nobody in this room is an egalitarian!" He laughed like he'd said something outrageously funny. "But still, very soon, you will be as rich and powerful as we are! You come to join the elite!"

Cap had answered. "We came because we were invited, Mr. Schoff. Egalitarianism is just some people talkin' and so far, rich and powerful ain't much more." Pete remembered him stuffing a cracker piled high with Caviar in his mouth and chewing it nice and slow. "We're sitting here in Switzerland, eating caviar and drinking expensive champagne, and that's nice. But I can do that in Cheyenne with people I actually like." He raised a hand and laughed. "Don't get me wrong, but I think President Trudeau is a clone of Macron and they are both identical assholes. So I don't like you." He pointed at the Canadian, "And any man who allows his country to be overrun by rapists and murderers who uphold a philosophy of slavery and genocide is beneath contempt, so my opinion of Ulf Kristersson is that he is a bigger asshole than Trudeau. So now we've got the pleasantries good and buried, how about we get down to business?"

Karl Schoff's patronizing smile had slipped into a scowl. "It never hurts to be polite and agreeable, Mr...." he trailed off.

"My friends call me Cap. You can call me captain. And I would have to disagree with you, Karl. Sometimes being polite and agreeable, when you are the poorest man in the room, can lead people to believe you are being servile and weak. I would hate you to get the wrong idea about that, Karl. We have something that you want real bad, because it can swing the balance of world power. Now the question we are asking is, 'How much can I get for this?' and the question you and your asshole friends are asking is, 'How little can I get away with paying?'"

He laughed, holding Karl Schoff's eye. "See, Karl, there is an elephant in the room, and I am looking at it and I can see it very clearly. You want me to describe it to you?"

"By all means."

"You have a choice, meet our price or, a couple of years down the line we will own you. The alternative is that you have us killed. But that will not only not solve your problem, it will cause you a lot of much more serious problems because obviously we foresaw that possibility and prepared for it. So, the elephant says you have to pay what we ask."

"And what do you ask?"

"US Federal funding for our research guaranteed over the next ten years. Guaranteed supply of the materials needed and, when the time comes, we take sixty percent of the price. Take it or leave it."

Schoff smiled and spread his hands wide as he hunched his shoulders. For good measure he raised his eyebrows too. Everything Was on the up, expansive. He turned to the Canadian, then to the Swede, "Gentlemen, it seems to me that Mr. Captain has made an exemplary case. I think I speak for all of us when I say that we accept."

The other two were less vocal and less enthusiastic, but Cap had read them right, right from the start, and he knew who called the shots in that room. WEFT called the shots in that room. Who called the shots at WEFT was something he and Cap would probably never know. Probably Karl Schoff didn't even know, though he was pretty close to the top of that pyramid.

Schoff was talking again. "You will see that there are no members of the United States Federal Administration present. So clearly it is impossible for me to arrange any kind of American Federal funding for whatever project it is you wish to promote. The best I can do is to have a word with some friends to see if I can engage anyone's interest in your," he paused, spread his hands and smiled, "project?"

For a moment Pete frowned and wondered if he was going crazy. Thirty seconds earlier they had it in the bag. Now – now he saw Cap nodding and smiling at the floor. He said, "We would be very grateful for that favor, Mr. Schoff. Though my friend and I are both fully aware that the moment we walk out that door you will forget we ever existed."

Schoff laughed like Cap had been really witty. "Don't be so pessimistic, my friend. Who knows, I have many friends and maybe somebody will think your idea is interesting. Don't be surprised if somebody calls you at noon in a couple of days. Have some more caviar, champagne!"

Cap stood. "Thanks, Mr. Schoff, but I'd rather have Godzilla wax my testicles and dribble sulfuric acid on them. We do appreciate the offer, though." He stood and looked at Pete. "Let's go, Pete, we have some drinking to do."

A footman opened the door for them and they stepped out into the burgundy corridor with its brass lamps and original 18th century paintings. As they made their way toward the elevators Pete turned to Cap and, with his face screwed into an expression of incomprehension, said, "Can you explain to me what the hell just happened in there?"

Cap stood nodding as the door of the elevator hissed open. They stepped inside and the doors closed. Then cap grinned at his old friend and said, "What happened, Pete, is that you and I just became very, very rich men. We just joined the billionaire club."

Two days later, at noon, the call had come. Cap had taken it. It had been from the Director of the Federal Office of the Environment. After a brief conversation with Cap he had flown directly to Jackson Hole and they had met, discretely, at the Jackson in town. The man was as gray and nondescript as his suit and his attaché case. After a brief luncheon, which he had paid for, they had taken him to the cabin and shown him their research – or that much of it as they wanted him to see, and right there and then he had opened the attaché case to reveal a computer with which he had opened them a bank account in Switzerland and transferred into it ten million dollars.

"This," he had said, is an account which is designated as 'of special interest', which means that neither the European Union nor any other official body such as Interpol or Europol knows it exists, let alone has access to it. The ten million is to get you started. As we see progress more will be added until you are ready to move. Then we'll start talking about serious figures."

The timeless fraction of a moment passed.

He went to say, "You can't," but he was overwhelmed by the beauty of the view through the glass. He was overwhelmed by the sudden knowledge that this place, Wyoming, was beautiful because it had not been completely soiled by the hand of Man. The grass grew as nature intended, the bison, the bears, the moose and the horses roamed as nature intended, and above, the eagles soared high into the dome of the sky. And as his mind soared with the eagle he was overwhelmed again, one last time, by a strange sensation. Time became timeless. There was a vast, incalculable stillness that might have lasted for an eternity. Then he simply winked out of existence. He never even knew he'd been shot in the back of the head.

DEAD HOT CHAPTER ONE

I smiled across the candle-lit table and said, "Your place or mine?" and my phone rang.

I have a special cell phone provided to me by the Office of the Director of Intelligence Networks, that allows me to silence all telephone calls, even turn off the telephone, and yet their calls will always get through. I gave a slow blink, said, "Sorry, I'll be very brief," I leaned back in my chair and put the phone to my ear.

The woman sitting opposite me was a PhD student specializing in deeply controversial Paleolithic cultures in Peru. Her eyebrows were as exquisite as her mind was, and she arched one of them at me as I said, "I am having dinner with the most fascinating woman I have ever met. What do you want? You have fifteen seconds and counting,"

Lovelock's throaty voice said, "I have twelve seconds and counting, you may or may not have a job in... uh...six seconds."

"What do you want?"

"You, in General Weisheim's office at the Pentagon in twenty-five minutes or less. Tell the Beautiful Brain to date an accountant next time. They are reliable and predictable, but they are so frustrated because they never get laid, they are surprisingly adventurous in bed."

"You just described me."

"Right." She hung up.

I looked across the table at the future Mrs. Dr. Mason slipping away. "Did I ever tell you," I said, "that I have a really interesting job?"

As she climbed into her cab fifteen minutes later she said, "Oh, Alex? I am going to be pretty tied up for the next few weeks, so, maybe," here she winked and smiled, "best if you don't call me, but I call you."

I watched her red tail lights disappear into the amber DC night, then hailed a cab of my own.

Thirty minutes later a lieutenant admitted me to General Weisheim's office on the fifth floor of the Pentagon. It was a big office that overlooked the sacred, Masonic, mystical inner pentagon gardens, a Subway and a Dunkin' Donuts. There was a huge, oak desk strategically placed so the general could keep an eye on Donut sales, a black leather chair that would have done justice to Darth Vader, a Stars and Stripes and a photograph of the president. That was all on the left.

On the right was a large, ethnic coffee table flanked by two sofas and three armchairs, one of which was a battered chesterfield and housed the general. One of the other chairs contained Nero. The sofas held a senior executive of Central Intelligence who is not appointed by the administration and who gives the director of the Company nightmares, a White House official who explains to incumbent presidents how to tell the difference between Israel and Palestine, whether to put the definite article 'the' in front of Ukraine, and the fact that London is not the capital of the fifty-first state. The military-industrial complex was also well represented by the CEO of a multi-billion dollar research and development facility in Nevada known as the Rat Lab, and the CEO of Gordon Alistair Avionics.

General Weisheim pointed to the last remaining armchair and said, "You're late."

I decided on a rictus instead of a smile and lowered myself into the chair. "The supermodel PhD student I just helped into a taxi said almost exactly the same thing, general, only she added 'too' to the construction."

"This is no time for wit, Mason. We are facing a serious problem." He jerked his chin at the head of the Rat Lab. "John, you want to kick off?"

John sucked in his cheeks and pursed his lips, then drummed a little tattoo on his knees with his hands.

"We conduct our most important projects in house, as you can imagine."

I waved my hand in the air, "Antigravity, cyborgs..."

"Exactly, but there are certain projects that come along sometimes that, for one reason or another, we allow other organizations or individuals to develop under our supervision and guidance until either they fail to fulfill their promise, or they realize that promise to a point where we need to step in and take over."

I glanced at Nero, but all his face said was that where I had been dragged away from a gorgeous genius with all the way up legs, he had been dragged away from a salmon fillet with sautéed fennel root and fresh oregano leaves, accompanied by a very cold Gewürztraminer; probably a Schlumberger, 2017.

His face said all that, which wasn't helpful. So to move things along a little, I said, "I think most of us here already knew that, John."

"This was the case with Pete Justin and a man who goes simply by the name Cap, though his real name is Hohóókee. He is from the Arapaho tribe. They were close friends and developed this project together."

"That's nice. What's the project?"

He glanced at the general, then at the nameless senior executive of Central Intelligence. He glanced at the White House official then at the CEO of Gordon Alistair Avionics. Nobody was offering him moral support. He took a deep breath.

"Up until now there have been only ten people on this planet who knew about this project. They were myself, the general, the White House representative, Mr. Smith of Gordon Alistair Avionics, a consortium of three trusted investors, Cap and Justin themselves. Now you and Mr. Nero will be privy to it.

"You said ten, that's just nine. Who's number ten."

"Pete Justin had a girlfriend. An Earth Sciences graduate from Arizona, But from what Cap tells me she did little more than make the coffee. I cannot stress to you enough how important this project is, and how important the most absolute secrecy is."

"Understood. Do you plan to tell us what the project is and why we are here at some point?"

"No."

"...what?"

"Yes and no."

"It gets better. Again, what?"

"I can give you some idea in general terms, but the details of the project must remain secret."

"Again, understood. I have been here close to twenty minutes. What do you say we get started? How about we start by you telling me why we *are* here?"

"I'm not liking your tone, son." It was the general, fishing a cigar from his breast pocket. I gave him a pleasant smile. "You know, sir, if I were part of your army, that would worry me."

I could feel Nero's eyes on me, but I was still mad at being cheated out of my date, so I didn't give a damn.

John cleared his throat. "If we could get back on track, in very general terms the aim of the project was to tap and utilize massive reserves of energy stored in and generated by the Yellowstone Caldera."

I narrowed my eyes. "This is the caldera which, if it erupts, will cause a global extinction event and wipe out humanity."

He sighed. "That is one of many theories."

"Yeah, but it's the only credible one. This is also the caldera which is due, or indeed overdue, for an eruption."

John nodded ponderously. "That, as I say, is one of *a number* of possibilities. There is an enormous amount of energy stored there, an inconceivable amount, and what Pete Justin and Cap were doing was to explore ways in which that energy could be tapped."

"And what were those methods?"

"That I cannot tell you, and neither do you need to know."

I turned to the general. "I am being briefed on, and told, what I need to know by the civilian CEO of a multinational defense contractor?"

He nodded. "Yup."

I looked at the Central Intelligence Übermensch but he just studied me back. I detected the heady aroma of absolute temporal power, and the expression of loathing on Nero's face told me I wasn't far wrong.

I looked back at the CEO of the Rat Lab. "OK, let's go through the looking glass, John. I, an employee of the Pentagon, am about to be briefed by the civilian CEO of a corporation which is not even American. And I have here a four star general and a Central Intelligence director who are in approval. Go ahead, John, brief me."

Everybody looked at the floor again, except the general who looked at Nero who was looking at me.

"Nero?"

Nero said, "Alex, shut up and listen to what Scrivener has to say."

"I am all ears, John."

"Just yesterday we receive a message from Cap to say that their array had picked up data which was very promising, and they would like to arrange a meeting. He said that Pete had been out of town but was returning imminently. We told him that as soon as Pete arrived they should let us know and we would go and have a look at the data. But -"

"But last night you received news that Peter Justin was dead or missing or both."

The silence in the room was deafening. The general growled, "How the hell did you know that?"

I gave the general a look you should never give a four star general. "Oh, come on," I said. "You broke up my date with a supermodel for this? I thought the Rat Lab only employed proven geniuses! Shall I tell you when I first suspected that your Cap friend had murdered Pete?" They all looked at each other. I went on, "When you said, and I quote, 'This was the case with Pete Justin and a man who goes simply by the name Cap, though his real name is Hohóókee. He is from the Arapaho tribe. They were close friends and developed this project together.' Now, let's keep it simple, if Pete and Hoho are pals and develop a project together which is of interest to the Rat Lab, and then the Rat Lab contact Nero and Mason at close to midnight for a meeting in the Pentagon, what are the odds that Hoho offed Pete?"

They all looked as though they really didn't like me, except Nero, who had started to smile. I went on.

"OK, geniae – is that the plural of genius? Geniae? Let's try another one. Pete and Hoho are looking at ways of tapping energy from the Yellowstone Caldera. Hoho kills Pete and the FBI are nowhere to be seen. Instead we have the military industrial complex out in force, with the industrial arm briefing the intelligence branch. From this do we deduce A that Pete and Hoho were planning to end world hunger, or B that there was some kind of National Security issue involved? National Security in this case embracing warmly and tenderly the capacity to annihilate large numbers of people in other countries."

I turned to the White House man. "By the way, while we are on the matter of annihilating large numbers of people, has he grasped yet that Palestine, Israel and Wales are different countries?"

The silence was leaden. It was Nero who broke it.

"Entertaining as this is, we need to move on. Officially, Alex, though Mr. Scrivener is briefing you, your instructions come from me, and my instructions come from the general."

"Super. And what are my instructions?"

John Scrivener sighed deeply, all the way down to his nervous toes.

"Let's take it in stages. First, lets find out what happened to Peter Justin -"

"You want to know if Cap Hoho has stolen the findings and is trying to sell them to Boris or the Chinese. If he has you want me to retrieve the goods and send him to apologize to his pal down in Hades."

"Mr. Mason, please."

"Yes or no?"

"Yes."

"What if it's too late and he has already sold the goods?"

Nero answered. "That is extremely unlikely. From what we know of Hohóokee he would be much more likely to offer it to us for sale and get us into a bidding war with the Russians and the Chinese. The fact that he has not as yet done so is of interest. If, however, you discover that the goods have been sold, to anyone other than us, you must inform me with the utmost speed and urgency."

"And this is all in Wyoming?"

"You fly to Jackson at six AM this morning."

I turned to Scrivener. "So why don't I just go, find this guy and beat him until he tells me what happened?"

He blinked uncomfortably at me. "Well, Mr. Mason, in the first place he may be telling the truth and he may be quite prepared to give us the da – the goods. In the second place, he is himself a dangerous man. He was a Marine and operative in Delta for many years. Lastly, and this is particularly true in Cap's case, we have learned the hard way that information gathered through torture is unreliable."

I grunted. "Does he know I am coming?"

"He knows a representative of the Federal Office of the Environment is flying out in the morning. You collect a car at Jackson Hole airport and he will meet you at the

Hotel Jackson. Nero will give you a file to study. There is not much in it, I'm afraid, but it's all we can give you."

I said: "In short, you want Pete and Cap's research, and you want to know who killed Pete."

"For now, that is the brief."

I stood and Nero heaved himself to his feet. "I have the Rolls," he said. "I'll take you."

On the way out he said, "I assume you have dined. My own dinner was interrupted."

"Yup, I have dined. For me it was the postprandial conversation that was interrupted."

"A wench, I assume."

"I was not kidding when I said she was a supermodel working for her PhD in the Paleolithic cultures of Peru."

His Rolls bleeped and he climbed in the back. I climbed in beside him and as the car pulled out of the parking garage he poured two twenty-one year old Bushmills.

"Controversial," he said, "Paleolithic cultures in Peru. However, in my experience, Alex, there is only one thing more dangerous than a beautiful woman."

I shook my head before sipping the whiskey. "The Yellowstone Caldera?"

He snorted. "Hardly. A beautiful woman who is also intelligent? Consider yourself fortunate to have had a narrow escape."

– END OF EXCERPT –

To see all purchasing options, please visit:
www.davidarcherbooks.com/dead-hot
www.blakebanner.com/dead-hot

ALSO BY DAVID ARCHER
& BLAKE BANNER

To see what else we have to offer, please
visit our respective websites.

www.davidarcherbooks.com
www.blakerbanner.com

Thank you once again for reading our work!

Made in the USA
Columbia, SC
01 December 2023